GRADUATION SUMMER

SV D P. 50

Everything I Want

By Cameron Dokey

HarperEntertainment

An Imprint of HarperCollins*Publishers*

A PARACHUTE PRESS BOOK

A PARACHUTE PRESS BOOK

Parachute Publishing, L.L.C.
156 Fifth Avenue
New York, NY 10010

Published by
HarperEntertainment
An Imprint of HarperCollins*Publishers*
10 East 53rd Street, New York, NY 10022-5299

TM & © 2004 Dualstar Entertainment Group, LLC

GRADUATION SUMMER books are created and produced by Parachute Publishing, L.L.C., in cooperation with Dualstar Publications, a division of Dualstar Entertainment Group, LLC., published by HarperEntertainment, an imprint of HarperCollins Publishers.

ISBN 0-06-072285-1

First printing: September 2004

Printed in the United States of America

Visit HarperEntertainment on the World Wide Web at
www.harpercollins.com

10 9 8 7 6 5 4 3 2 1

CHAPTER ONE

Southern California, we have a problem.

Big-time.

Mary-Kate Olsen stood in the center of her bedroom, hands on her hips, her bright blue eyes doing a quick survey as she turned her head from side to side. At least she *thought* she was in the center of her room. It was kind of hard to tell, since the room itself was pretty much buried under all her . . .

There was really only one word for it.

Stuff, she thought.

Not that that should be mistaken for a diss. It was all really great stuff. The trouble was, its overall greatness was part of the problem. Mary-Kate and her sister, Ashley, were leaving for college on the East Coast first thing in the morning. Super-organized Ashley was already packed—had been for days. But Mary-Kate was still struggling after a solid week of *attempting* to pack.

What we have here is a heart-brain failure to communicate, she decided as she climbed over two open suitcases, half a dozen piles of sweaters, and a stack of CDs on her way to the bed. She sat down with a *whoosh* and hugged the pillow her mom had given her for her last birthday to her chest. Her brain kept downloading useful information about what *not* to pack, which her heart kept right on ignoring.

Take this pillow, for instance, she thought. Her mom had discovered it at a local antique shop. It was quirky and fun, and Mary-Kate absolutely loved it. It was also . . . large. That was the part Mary-Kate had to acknowledge. She tossed it into the nearest open suitcase. *Yep. Pretty much what I thought.*

Her fabulous, wacky pillow took up a third of a suitcase all on its own. The practical thing to do would be to leave it behind. But how could she bear to do such a thing? She loved that pillow. It made her smile every time she saw it.

Maybe I could have one suitcase that's just personal mementos, she thought. That way she could also take along her collection of wildlife posters. A girl had to put something on her dorm-room walls, after all. And if she took the posters, she might as well take along the . . .

Stop! she told herself as she shot to her feet. *Stop! Stop! STOP!* This was precisely what she'd been doing for the entire past week and it was all too obvious it hadn't gotten her very far.

"Don't go there, Mary-Kate," she murmured. "Oh, great! Now I'm talking to myself."

Plainly the time had come to call for reinforcements.

Suddenly inspired, she hopped over a pile of socks to reach her desk. She started typing on her laptop.

Mary★★★Kate invites AshleyO to Instant Message.

```
Mary***Kate: This is special agent MKO
    calling special agent AO. Surrounded
    by enemy forces. Immediate assistance
    desperately needed. Help. Help.
    HELP! :0
```

It only took moments for Ashley's response to appear.

```
AshleyO: RU joking? Thought your mission
    was almost accomplished.
Mary***Kate: No way. It's impossible!
AshleyO: Ha-ha. Very funny. :-P
Mary***Kate: Hurry! They're attacking!
    I can't hold out much longer!
    Arrghhhhh!
```

"Ever consider *not* trying to pack every single thing you own?" Ashley inquired dryly a few moments later from the bedroom doorway. From the look on her sister's face, Mary-Kate could see that Ashley was having a hard time not laughing.

"For heaven's sake, Mary-Kate!" Ashley exclaimed now. "What have you been doing in here all this time?

We leave tomorrow morning, in case you've forgotten."

"Not likely," Mary-Kate replied. "And I've been trying—honestly I have. But every time I decide to leave something out, it somehow ends up right back in the take-me-with-you-to-college pile."

"I think you mean piles," Ashley said, giving the closest one a poke with her Skecher.

"What *I* think," Mary-Kate answered dramatically, "is that my possessions have developed minds of their own. I could really use some help here, Ash. I don't know how to eliminate anything."

Ashley sighed. "Just pick a pile and follow through," she said. She took two steps into the room, which was about as far as she could get without running into something. "Take these sweaters, for example," she continued, pointing at her feet. "Do you actually need six *piles* of them? The weather will still be pretty nice when we get to Lawton College. It's only September, after all. And we'll be back here for Thanksgiving break."

"But what if there's a sudden cold snap?" Mary-Kate protested. "Ashley, we're talking New England! They have power outages. It *snows*. Those sweaters might be the only things standing between us and a future as the popsicle sisters."

"Mary-Kate . . ." Ashley began, but by now her sister was on a roll.

"You could take a few of them for me, couldn't

you?" she pleaded as she hopped over the CDs, scooped up the nearest two piles of sweaters, and thrust them into Ashley's somewhat unwilling arms.

"Mary-Kate . . ." Ashley began again. This time she was interrupted by the sudden trilling of Mary-Kate's alarm clock.

"Omigosh!" Mary-Kate yelped. She spun around, jumping over a lineup of shoes to reach her bedside table and silence the alarm. "Is that the right time? How did it get so late? I'm never going to make it. I have to go!"

"Wait a minute," Ashley protested as Mary-Kate leapt back over the shoes and bounded past her, out the bedroom door, and down the hall. "Go where? Late for what?"

"To the beach. Date with Trevor." Mary-Kate's voice floated back up the stairs. "See ya when I get home. Thanks for helping me out, Ash. I really appreciate it."

There was the sound of the front door *swooshing* open, then closing with a bang. Ashley was left standing in the doorway of Mary-Kate's room, cradling an armload of her sister's sweaters and shaking her head.

Mary-Kate strikes again. How did her sister do it? Ashley wondered. She'd come to Mary-Kate's room determined to convince her to be practical about packing, and ended up agreeing to take two enormous piles of sweaters for her! Not that she seriously objected to helping out. That's what sisters were for. Within reason, of course.

And that's the problem, Ashley thought. When it came to *reason,* she and her sister didn't exactly see eye to eye. Mary-Kate was almost totally spontaneous, while Ashley preferred a more organized approach to life.

Oh, well, she thought now as she wandered back down the hall to her own room, the sweaters still in her arms. She probably *did* have space for a few more things. And she'd never in a million years suggest that Mary-Kate miss her last big date with her boyfriend, Trevor Reynolds, to wrestle with packing issues. A girl had to have priorities, after all. Saying good-bye to the guy you liked ranked right at the top of anyone's to-do list, even Ashley's.

She knelt by her suitcases, opened the one she knew was the least full, and made some rearrangements to fit Mary-Kate's sweaters in.

There, she thought as she zipped the suitcase closed. *That's done.* She considered returning to Mary-Kate's room to finish things up while Mary-Kate was out with Trevor, then rejected the idea. They'd never learn to be independent at college if Ashley did all of Mary-Kate's packing for her before they even left home!

Independence was an important issue for both Olsen girls. In fact, they'd been so serious about it that they'd convinced their parents to let them make the trip to Lawton College on their own. The school had a shuttle van that would meet arriving students at the airport. Their parents would visit for a special family weekend at school in November, after which they'd all go home together to California for Thanksgiving break.

The girls had also decided against rooming together, though they had asked to be assigned to the same dorm. Naturally, both sisters wanted great relationships with their new roomies. Wasn't being best friends with your roommate part of what college was all about?

At the thought of her new roommate, Zoe Hanover, Ashley felt her stomach give a little clutch.

When the girls had filled out their housing applications, there'd been a place on the form to provide your current address if you wanted to get in touch with your future roommate ahead of time. After Zoe and Ashley had exchanged a few phone calls and e-mails—and survived a horrible miscommunication about their room's color scheme—Ashley had decided to send Zoe one of those "All About Me" quizzes that always made the rounds in e-mail.

The list of questions covered everything from favorite color, band, movie, and last book read to more abstract things, like what did you want to be when you grew up, who's had the most influence on who you are today, and what's the one thing about yourself that you'd want a new friend to know. To her delight, Zoe had responded in kind. Ashley had been amazed to see how similar their backgrounds were. Like Ashley, Zoe had been her senior class's valedictorian.

But after that promising beginning, contact with Zoe had slowed to a trickle, then stopped. Ashley had tried to tell herself that it was okay. The best way to get to know a person was face-to-face, after all. But as the days went by, the thing she'd been forced to face was the truth: She was worried about her relationship with her new roommate. Worried about her relationship with a person she hadn't even met yet!

If that wasn't obsessing, she didn't know what was.

Okay, Ashley, she told herself now. *If you're going to obsess, at least do it over something useful, like your class schedule.* That was something over which she might have some control, after all.

Reaching for the folder in which she kept her careful notes about the classes she hoped to take, Ashley curled up on her bed to review them for what even she would have to admit was about the millionth time. At the rate she was going, she'd be able to draw a map of the campus and include the route she'd take from one class to the next.

Actually, that's not a bad idea, she thought. Even on a small college campus, Ashley was willing to bet new students got lost. *But that isn't going to happen to Ms. Ashley Olsen. No sirree.*

Because, she wasn't just O for *Obsessed.* She was also O for *Organized*!

AshleyO invites Felicity_girl and Claude18 to Instant Message!

```
AshleyO: All set for Operation Big
    Surprise?
Claude18: Be there with bells on!
Felicity_Girl: No! No! She'll hear u.
    That'll ruin everything!
Claude18: Ha-ha. MK got her packing
    done yet?
AshleyO : Don't ask. :(
Felicity_Girl: Uh oh.
AshleyO : U can say that again. Gotta
    dash. See u u-no when.
```

CHAPTER TWO

This is absolutely perfect, Trevor," Mary-Kate said.

From his position beside the barbecue pit, Trevor Reynolds looked up and grinned.

"Nothing's too good for the girl of my dreams," he declared dramatically as he slid the hot dog he'd been roasting over the fire off the cooking stick and into a bun. Brown eyes dancing, he held it up. "Didn't you say you wanted extra onions?"

"Eeewww!" Mary-Kate exclaimed with a scrunch of her nose.

"Oh, that's right. Now I remember," Trevor continued as he got up from his crouch and walked toward the blanket where Mary-Kate was sitting. "You said you wanted sauerkraut."

"Sauerkraut is not a food," Mary-Kate informed him as he plopped down beside her, sliding the hot dog onto a waiting paper plate. "It's an alien life-form."

Trevor laughed, and Mary-Kate felt a little squeeze around her heart. She absolutely loved spending time with him! How was she going to get along without him when she went away to college? On impulse she leaned forward, snagged a handful of Trevor's T-shirt, and pulled him toward her. She saw his eyes widen in delighted surprise just before their lips met.

"Well," Trevor said when the kiss was over. "If that's the way you feel about my cooking, maybe I should consider going to culinary school."

Mary-Kate put an open palm over Trevor's face and pushed him backward with a laugh. One of the things she'd always loved best about Trevor—even before they'd started dating and had just been best buds—was his sense of humor.

"Where's that dinner you promised me?" she asked.

Trevor pushed himself up and snuck a quick kiss. "Coming right up," he said.

For the next few moments the two busied themselves with happily consuming the perfect picnic: hot dogs and potato salad. The concept of spending their last date on the beach had been Mary-Kate's idea. But it was Trevor who'd suggested making it a picnic. Though the evening wasn't all that cold, the couple had built a fire in one of the barbecue pits.

Much better than candlelight as far as Mary-Kate was concerned.

"Okay, I admit it. I am now officially stuffed," Trevor said. He scooted over to sit beside Mary-Kate, leaning back against one of the big rocks that lined the beach, and stretched his legs out in front of him.

"Me, too," Mary-Kate said. Trevor put an arm around her and tugged her in close. "Now I'm really going to have to pay attention to what I pack. Otherwise I'll be over my weight limit for the flight!"

"How's the packing going?" Trevor inquired.

"Slowly," Mary-Kate admitted with a rueful laugh. "I always thought I had a pretty good imagination, but I just can't seem to 'imagine' life without all the things I'm used to."

Including you, she thought.

As if he'd read her thoughts, Trevor tilted her chin up and gave her a gentle kiss.

"That's called moving on," he said softly.

"I know that," Mary-Kate said. "I honestly do. It's just . . ."

"Just what?" Trevor prompted after a moment.

"It's not like I'm going away forever," Mary-Kate said. "And I know things here won't stay the same, but . . ."

"You're worried about us, aren't you?" Trevor interrupted quietly.

"Of course not," Mary-Kate said swiftly.

Okay, Trevor, your cue, she thought.

This was the moment he was supposed to say something like *me, neither.* Then Mary-Kate could feel she understood how things would be when they were apart without actually having to discuss the situation. They'd already had enough miscommunication about their relationship over the summer. But when Trevor didn't answer, the silence between them stretched.

"Okay, well, yeah. Maybe. Sort of," Mary-Kate acknowledged. "We never really settled on what will happen while we're three thousand miles and three hours' time difference apart."

Unlike Mary-Kate and Ashley, Trevor was staying on the West Coast to attend a great art school.

"Will we—you know—see other people? That kind of stuff," Mary-Kate struggled on.

"Do you want to?" Trevor asked quickly, and Mary-Kate could feel the way the arm around her shoulders tensed abruptly.

She pulled in a deep breath. "No, I don't. I can't imagine so much as looking at another guy now that I've found you."

Without warning Trevor dropped his chin down to rest on the top of her head. "How come you always know the right thing to say?" he asked.

Mary-Kate felt a bubble of perfect happiness swell inside her chest. Trevor felt the same way she did! He didn't want to date new people at college!

"I don't know," she answered as she turned her face up for a kiss. "Just lucky, I guess."

Trevor smiled, his lips a breath away from hers. "That makes two of us."

•   •   •

Mary-Kate's heart sang with happiness all the way home. She and Trevor had sorted out the sticky issue of what would happen while she was away at college. Not that long-distance relationships were a piece of cake. They could be complicated and tricky, or so every single article Mary-Kate had ever read on the topic informed her. But all those articles were missing one thing as far as she was concerned: the Trevor factor. What the two of them shared was truly special. Surely that had to count for something.

"Guess this is the last time we'll be doing this for a while, huh?" Trevor commented now as, beneath the front porch light, he pulled Mary-Kate into his arms.

Mary-Kate smiled up at him. "Guess you'll just have to make the most of it then, won't you?"

"Oh, yeah," Trevor said. "In fact, I was pretty much counting on it."

Mary-Kate's smile got a little bit wider. "So what are you waiting for?"

Trevor's kiss was deep and soulful, as if he was trying to put everything he felt into this one kiss, this one moment. Mary-Kate responded in kind, then rested her head against Trevor's chest when the kiss was done. She could feel the way his heart beat in firm, even strokes.

"I'd better let you go in," Trevor finally said. "Don't you have to get a pretty early start tomorrow?"

"Right after breakfast," Mary-Kate acknowledged. "And I do have to finish packing first."

The two fell silent, facing each other. Then Trevor lifted a gentle hand to Mary-Kate's cheek.

"See you at Thanksgiving," he said. "Wear a bow when you get off the plane so I'll know it's you."

With that he turned and bounded off down the front walk.

Mary-Kate stayed on the porch, her gaze following Trevor's every move as he started his Jeep, lifted his hand in a farewell wave, then zoomed off down the block.

This is it. It's really happening, she thought.

This was the last time she'd see the guy she loved for nearly three months. Tomorrow morning she was leaving for college.

Mary★★★Kate invites AshleyO to Instant Message!

Mary★★★Kate: Well, it's official. It's
true love 4ever.

AshleyO: So that means you'll be playing
the field at college?

Mary★★★Kate: Very funny.

AshleyO: Seriously, Trev's a great guy.
I am happy 4 u. Now finish packing!
>:-)

Mary★★★Kate: Nag. Nag. I'm going to
bed. Us girls in love need our beauty
sleep! See you in the morning!

CHAPTER THREE

Mary-Kate Olsen!" Ashley exclaimed. "Please tell me you're not planning to pack last year's Halloween costume."

Mary-Kate looked up from where she'd been trying to stuff the slinky black cat costume into the front pocket of one of her suitcases.

"I don't see why not," she said. "Don't they have Halloween on the East Coast?"

"Mary-Kate," Ashley said, her voice a perfect imitation of their mother's when she was pushed to just about her limit.

"All right, all right," Mary-Kate said before her sister could go on. "It's not like it was going to fit anyhow."

By resorting to what Mary-Kate considered extreme nagging tactics, Ashley had managed to get the number of Mary-Kate's suitcases down to four. To that Mary-Kate would add her laptop and a rolling duffel bag as carry-ons. Her favorite framed photograph of Trevor was secured in bubble wrap and nestled carefully in the very top of the duffel.

"Oookaay," Mary-Kate said now. She made a quick motion with her hands as if dusting them off. "I'm not sure I believe this myself, but I think I might be done."

She turned to Ashley, her blue eyes managing to twinkle with laughter and express her gratitude all at once. Ashley *had* been pretty great, particularly considering the fact that Mary-Kate had dragged her out of bed at six o'clock in the morning.

"What's my time, coach?"

Ashley consulted her watch. "Seven days, two hours, thirty-seven minutes, and eight seconds," she announced. "Congratulations. I think it's a new world record."

"Absolutely." Mary-Kate nodded. "Too bad it's for slowness!"

"Hey, at least you get an award for something."

"Thank you so much, Ms. Valedictorian."

The front doorbell rang, the sound echoing through the quiet house.

"Boy!" Mary-Kate exclaimed. "Who'd come by at eight o'clock in the morning?"

"Only one way to find out," Ashley remarked, trying not to grin.

The doorbell rang again, more insistently this time.

"Girls?" Their mother's voice floated up the stairs. "Will one of you get that, please?"

"You did something, didn't you?" Mary-Kate asked as an incredible thought occurred to her.

Ashley's face went completely blank. "I'm sure I don't know what you're talking about."

"You did!" Mary-Kate exclaimed with a whoop. "You did do something. Not only that, I'll bet I know what."

She dashed down the stairs as a steady, rhythmic pounding commenced on the front door. Mary-Kate pulled it open to reveal her best friend, Claudia Pierce, and Ashley's best friend, Felicity Lopez, standing side by side.

"It *is*!" Mary-Kate cried. "You guys! This is so great!" She arched up on tiptoe, trying to see over their shoulders.

Claudia shot Felicity a quick wink. "What's the matter?" she asked Mary-Kate. "Expecting someone else?"

"It's just that I was wondering . . . " Mary-Kate began.

Suddenly Trevor's head appeared between Claudia's and Felicity's. With a squeal of delight, Mary-Kate launched herself into his arms, Felicity and Claudia scrambling out of the just way in the nick of time.

"Hey, you guys. Come on in," Ashley said as she appeared in the doorway. "It's so great that you could make it."

"As if we would have missed it," Felicity said. She and Ashley exchanged a quick hug. "Particularly when your mom's pancakes are involved."

"Pancakes?" Mary-Kate all but squealed. "Mom's making pancakes? They're my faves. Oh, geez. I'm getting all sentimental. I might have to cry."

"If you do, I get your pancakes," Trevor said.

"Wait a minute. I think I'm about to recover."

Trevor grinned. "I thought so."

"I could use a little help setting the table out here!" the girls' mother sang out.

"Coming, Mom," Mary-Kate called.

The friends all trooped toward the dining room. Mary-Kate gave Ashley's shoulders a quick squeeze. "Thanks," she said. "You are absolutely the best."

"I don't suppose you'd care to put that in writing?" Ashley asked with a smile.

"Omigosh!" Mary-Kate suddenly exclaimed, and she watched in satisfaction as Ashley's eyes widened. "I *knew* there was something I meant to do before I left for college!"

"What?" Ashley demanded.

"Learn to write!"

"Well, I guess this is it," Ashley said, wishing her stomach didn't feel quite so funny all of a sudden. Of course, that *could* be from all the pancakes she'd had for breakfast, but she didn't think so. She knew precisely why her stomach felt like an Olympic gymnast performing on the parallel bars.

This was really it. In just another moment she and

Mary-Kate would pass through the airport security checkpoint and officially be on their way to college.

"Call us when you get in, okay?" their mother said for the twentieth time as she caught first Ashley, then Mary-Kate in a fierce hug. "I know everything's going to be just fine, but I'll worry anyway until I hear from you. I can't help it. It's my job as your mother."

"Of course we'll call, Mom," Mary-Kate promised. "What was the phone number again?"

The girls' mother gave a watery laugh. "Brat," she said as she wiped moisture from her eyes. At the sight of her mother's tears, Ashley felt her own threaten. She didn't have to look at Mary-Kate to know she was feeling the same way.

"Don't just stand there," their mother said, elbowing their father in the ribs. "Say something."

"I hope the flight is smooth and neither of you gets airsick," Mr. Olsen said with a perfectly straight face.

Her tears forgotten in sudden laughter, Ashley launched herself into her father's arms.

Mr. Olsen hugged the girls to him, Ashley on one side, Mary-Kate on the other.

"The thing I'd really like to say," he went on in his deep, quiet voice, "is how enormously proud I am of you both. Though I'd like you to keep in mind that, if you mess up after all the college tuition I'm paying, you're both grounded for life."

"We'll be sure to keep that in mind, Dad," Ashley promised.

"Okay then," Mr. Olsen said as he let them go.

The girls exchanged one final hug with their mother, then turned to face the security checkpoint. Ashley felt Mary-Kate's hand clasp her own.

"You ready to do this?" Mary-Kate asked.

"Absolutely!" Ashley answered. All of a sudden her stomach felt just fine. Her sister was with her, their parents were behind them. What on earth could possibly go wrong?

"Lawton College, here we come!"

Mary***Kate invites Claude18 to Instant Message!

Mary***Kate: Claude, u gotta help me!

Claude18: Hey, grrl. U sound desperate. Where are u?

Mary***Kate: Waiting to board the plane. Look, I need you to mail me some stuff.

Claude18: OK. Like what?

Mary***Kate: Like all the stuff Ashley made me leave behind! I want my Halloween costume. People at Lawton DESERVE to see me in that Halloween costume.

Claude18: Couldn't agree more. U R on!

CHAPTER FOUR

Whatever you do, do *not* panic," Ashley advised.

Mary-Kate gazed around in dismay. "Does that include yelling for help?"

Two flights and one shuttle ride later, the sisters were at long last standing on their new college campus in front of what was supposed to be their dorm. Despite the fading daylight, it looked as lovely as it had in the catalogue. Originally a mansion from the Victorian era, it was a tall and stately brick building with sparkling leaded windows and a big brass knocker adorning the front door.

Unfortunately, the knocker wasn't the only thing the door was wearing. Ribbons of yellow hazard tape zigzagged across it, giving the dormitory the appearance of a crime scene. An enormous sign lettered in bold black letters declared:

HAZARDOUS AREA. DO NOT ENTER UNDER ANY CIRCUMSTANCES.

"How about whining?" Mary-Kate asked now. "I

know it's off-limits as a rule, but where are we supposed to go? What are we supposed to do?"

"Olsen," a female voice suddenly announced.

Ashley turned to see a tall young woman with dark brown hair striding toward them purposefully, a clipboard clutched like a shield to her chest. She was dressed in faded blue jeans and a crisply pressed oxford-cloth shirt.

"Are you the Olsen sisters, Mary-Kate and Ashley?" she asked.

"I'm Ashley, and this is Mary-Kate," Ashley said as she extended her hand. The young woman took it, her grip brisk and firm.

"I'm Sharon Newton, your RA—resident advisor," she said. "Or I will be your RA, just as soon as we get this mess under control."

"What happened?" Mary-Kate inquired.

"Water damage," Sharon Newton said. "A water main burst yesterday. There are problems all over this part of town. We're hoping the damage to the dorm isn't too extensive, but, naturally, making sure the building is safe for students is our first priority. Until that's done . . ." Her voice trailed off.

"What happens to us in the meantime?" Mary-Kate inquired. "All of us who are supposed to live here, I mean. How many students does this dorm hold?"

"About twenty-five," Sharon answered. "Most are double rooms, but there are a couple of singles and one three-person suite. We're finding you all accommodations where we can, trying to keep students as close to campus as possible. You guys actually have it pretty good." She pivoted on one heel and pointed to a row of townhouses directly across the street. "You'll be right over there. The townhouse with the mums in the window boxes."

"That's fantastic!" Ashley declared.

Though not as old as the building that would eventually be their dorm, the townhouses were also built of brick and very definitely charming. Ashley particularly liked the riot of fall colors provided by the chrysanthemums that filled the white window boxes on either side of the big front door.

"There are a couple of things you two should know about the place before I give you both the keys," Sharon Newton said. "First and foremost, the house belongs to a professor who's away this semester on sabbatical."

"A professor's house!" Mary-Kate exclaimed. "Bet that doesn't happen very often."

"You'd be right," Sharon acknowledged. "You were chosen because your academic records—Ashley's in particular—demonstrate a high degree of reliability."

"In other words, rule number one is: Don't Trash the Professor's Place," Mary-Kate commented.

"Also rules two through ten," Sharon said with a smile. "Never forget you're in the home of a Lawton professor, and don't forget that you might end up in one of his classes sometime down the road!"

"Yikes! Okay, we'll remember," Mary-Kate promised.

Sharon consulted her clipboard for a moment. "I see by my notes that your roommates, Zoe Hanover and Madison Andrews, have already moved in. Hope you like the rooms they chose. Let me give you your keys, and you'll be all set. Oh, and one more thing: Professor Donovan specifically requested that no one enter his home office or use his phone. I assume you've both got cells, so that shouldn't be a problem."

"Right," Ashley said. "But thanks for letting us know."

"I think that's it, then," the Sharon said. She slid an enormous leather shoulder bag to the ground, then knelt down beside it. A moment later she produced an envelope with OLSEN written in crisp, precise handwriting across the top. She opened it and tipped two keys out into her palm.

"Here you go," she said, as she rose to her feet. "The same key opens both the front door lock and the deadbolt. Any questions?"

"How can we contact you if we need you?" Ashley inquired.

At this, Sharon Newton reached into her shirt pocket and extracted two white business cards. "I had these made up for all my freshmen. It has my cell number and e-mail address," she said. "I'll do my best to see how you guys are settling in, but things might be pretty hectic the first few days. I've got a lot of students to get straightened away between now and when school starts."

"Don't worry about us," Mary-Kate said quickly. "I'm sure we'll be fine."

"If you have any questions or concerns, don't hesitate to be in touch," Sharon said. "I guess that's it, unless you want some help with those bags."

She eyed the pile of luggage with a look that Ashley could only describe as dubious. She was just pulling in a breath to accept Sharon's offer when Mary-Kate spoke up.

"Oh, that's all right," she said breezily. "We got them this far. I'm sure we can get them across the street. It's only a little farther."

"If you say so," Sharon said just as her cell phone began to warble. "Nice to have met you both. I'm sure I'll see you soon."

With that, she strode off down the street at the same brisk pace with which she'd approached, cell phone pressed to one ear.

Mary-Kate picked up what Ashley couldn't help but notice were the lightest two of her suitcases.

"What are you waiting for?" Mary-Kate asked. "Come on. Let's go check things out."

With that, she hurried across the street as fast as the

suitcases would allow. Ashley followed more slowly, pulling Mary-Kate's heavier two suitcases behind her, leaving her own outside the dorm for the moment. She'd just reached the sidewalk, with Mary-Kate halfway up the front walk, when the door to the townhouse burst open and a girl their age dashed out.

She was about the same height as the twins themselves, but all resemblance ended there. Her hair was dark. The cut was short and angular, almost as if she'd gone to a barber shop. Tiny gold hoops winked in her ears.

In contrast to her boyish haircut she wore a skin-tight black camisole topped by an oversized white shirt with a froth of ruffles down the front. Slim black bells and a pair of chunky shoes completed the ensemble. She had an open, appealing face and a smile about a mile wide.

Without any hesitation, she headed straight for Mary-Kate. "You have *got* to be Mary-Kate Olsen!" she cried. "You look exactly like the picture you sent. I'm your roommate, Madison Andrews. Wait till you see the room I scored for us."

Instantly she launched into a breathless description, her words tumbling over one another so quickly that not even Mary-Kate could get a word in edgewise.

"It's on the main floor," Madison said. "Good thing, with those suitcases, I'm guessing. What did you do, pack your entire wardrobe? It has a window seat, a set of French doors, and it's absolutely *humongous*! You have *got* to come and see it right this minute!"

"If you say so," Mary-Kate said enthusiastically when Madison finally paused for breath. "I'll be back to help in just a sec, okay?" she said to Ashley.

"Sure, fine, go ahead," Ashley panted. "I'm Ashley, by the way."

"Madison Andrews," Mary-Kate's roommate said. "It's nice to meet you. You and Zoe are upstairs."

Madison angled her head up toward the second story. Ashley followed suit and thought she saw the curtains move in a window upstairs.

"Do you want me to call her?" Madison asked.

"No, thanks," Ashley said, fighting back a pang of disappointment. Madison had been so excited to meet Mary-Kate that she'd dashed outside to meet her. Although Zoe had been the first to contact Ashley during the summer, apparently her future roommate didn't feel the same way anymore.

"Back in a flash," Mary-Kate promised. Then she and Madison sprinted up the front walk.

"Wait!" Ashley called. "Mary-Kate, at least take the bags you brought over!" But it was plain her sister didn't hear her. Mary-Kate and Madison had already vanished into the townhouse. Now thoroughly out of sorts, Ashley stared at the lineup of her sister's suitcases filling the sidewalk.

"At least they're all on this side of the street," she muttered under her breath. And now that they were, Mary-Kate could just take it from here on out!

Ashley was just turning to recross the street and retrieve her own luggage when the door to the townhouse next door opened, then closed with a brisk snap. Ashley spun toward the sound. Standing on the porch next door was a man she judged to be in his early thirties. Dark hair flopped casually across his forehead, but his expression was intense. In one hand he held a bulging leather briefcase.

"I simply can*not* handle these noisy interruptions," he announced, glaring at Ashley from under his dark eyebrows. "I must have quiet time. You might not care if I get tenure, but I do!"

With that, he marched down his front steps and strode away, his long legs eating up the sidewalk.

Ashley sighed. The household was off to a bad start with their new neighbor already, and they'd only just arrived.

"Come on, Ash," she muttered to herself as she finally managed to retrieve her own belongings. "Look on the bright side. You made it to college!"

Now all she had to do was to unpack, relax, and meet her new roommate. Surely all the crises of her first day at college were over!

AshleyO invites Felicity_girl to Instant Message!

AshleyO: The Olsen has landed!

Felicity_girl: Congrats! How's it
    going?

AshleyO: U mean aside from the fact
    that the pipes in our dorm exploded?

Felicity_girl: Yikes! :-0

AshleyO: U know it! Temporary housing
    very cool, though.

Felicity_girl: Excellent. Keep me
    posted.

CHAPTER FIVE

I know our room is smaller than Mary-Kate and Madison's," Zoe Hanover said, her tone slightly defensive, as if Ashley had complained about the choice.

"But it has a much better view of campus," Zoe continued, "and, besides, we'll only be here until the dorm thing gets straightened out. You know that view of the quad featured on the cover of the Lawton catalogue? That's it, right over there." She pointed out the window. "Is that cool or what?"

"Very cool," Ashley agreed, wishing she could think of a more interesting remark. Though she was often comfortable with new people right away, something about Zoe made it hard for Ashley to feel as if she was making any progress.

Like Madison's, Zoe's looks were a big contrast to the Olsens'. But where Madison was small and dark-haired, Zoe was a tall redhead. Ashley was willing to bet she was good at every sport there was, including some Ashley didn't even know about!

"Of course the person in the bed closest to the

window really has the *best* view," Zoe went on now. She plunked herself down upon it, folding her long legs up underneath her. "I've already claimed it. I hope you don't mind. We'd already lost out on the room downstairs, and I *did* get here first."

"Of course I don't mind," Ashley said politely. She moved to the bed nearest the door, which she now knew to be hers, and she heaved her suitcases up onto it. A sudden thump, followed by a burst of laughter, drifted up the stairs.

"What's *in* here?" she heard Madison exclaim. "Rocks?"

"How did you know?" Mary-Kate quipped.

"Well," Zoe said, shifting on her bed a bit as a second burst of laughter rolled upstairs. "Those two seem to be hitting it off."

"They do, don't they?" Ashley said, wishing she could say the same about Zoe and herself. *It's probably just jetlag slowing things down,* she thought. *We hit it off pretty well by e-mail over the summer.*

"I unpacked right away, too," Zoe said into the suddenly awkward silence. "Can you believe how alike we are? My friends back home were kind of worried. They were afraid you and I might compete because we have such similar backgrounds. But I don't think that's going to happen, do you?"

"Of course not," Ashley said firmly.

"Of course not," Zoe echoed with a laugh that was

just a shade too loud. "I mean, these are the same friends who kept telling me how tough going away to college would be. Most of my best friends stayed in-state. They'll be able to go home on weekends and stuff if they want.

"Even my dad got into the act. He kept reminding me I wasn't going to be the big fish in the small pond anymore. Instead, I was going to be a small fish in a big pond. Not that I'm worried or anything," she went on quickly. "I'm sure everything's going to be just fine."

"Of course it is," Ashley said, privately appalled. Unlike her own parents, Zoe's family didn't sound all that excited about Zoe's college plans.

Ashley pulled a pile of carefully folded pants out of her suitcase and moved to the chest of drawers nearest the head of her bed. Like the rest of the furniture in the house, the bureau looked old. It was made of beautifully polished wood and had a mirror attached to the top.

"Oh, I took that one," Zoe said just as Ashley pulled open the top drawer and discovered that on her own. "I know it's a *little* closer to your bed, but it was so pretty, I couldn't resist it! You don't mind, do you?"

"Not at all," Ashley said through slightly clenched teeth.

She turned and moved to the second chest of drawers. It was all the way across the room, *much* closer to Zoe's bed than Ashley's own.

Just chill out, Ash. It's only for a few days, she reminded herself. *Once we're in the dorm, everyone will have the exact same furniture.* Swiftly she stowed away the first armload of clothes, then returned to the suitcase for another.

"I was thinking we should set up the stereo on your dresser," Zoe informed her, "since mine has that mirror thing on top. I really like to listen to music while I fall asleep, don't you? I told you about that, right? And remember how I always sleep with the window open? All that fresh air is good for the brain cells!"

At precisely that moment Ashley realized something. Her brain cells were sending her a message she couldn't ignore. They hurt. In fact, every single part of her head hurt. Right down to the hair she was desperately trying not to pull out.

"Are you okay, Ashley?" Zoe asked suddenly. "You look—I don't know—funny or something."

"I'm *fine*," she said firmly. "I'm *absolutely fine*. I'd just like to get my unpacking finished."

Preferably in peace and quiet, she added to herself. After fifteen minutes with her new roommate, all she wanted to do was to be left alone.

So much for thinking nothing else could possibly go wrong that day!

"This is just the best," Mary-Kate declared, as she stood in the center of their room. "In fact, it's totally going to spoil me for moving into the dorm!"

"I hear that!" Madison said with a smile.

As in Ashley and Zoe's room upstairs, Mary-Kate's and Madison's beds, chests of drawers, and desks were pushed flush against the walls. Unlike upstairs, however, the interior of this room felt spacious and open, even with Mary-Kate's suitcases in the center. At the room's far end a cozy seat was tucked into a bay window. Beside it French doors opened out onto a lush garden.

"Oh, well," Mary-Kate said enthusiastically. "At least it's ours for a couple of days. Way to go!"

"Think nothing of it," Madison replied. "All in a day's work for Madison Andrews, Super-roomie. I'm thinking of having a T-shirt made."

The girls laughed easily.

"So, what are you going to unpack first?" Madison asked as she flopped down on the window seat. "I notice you've got plenty to choose from."

"Don't *you* start on my suitcases!" Mary-Kate exclaimed. "I almost didn't make it down to four! But to answer your question . . ."

She dropped to her knees beside her duffel bag, unzipped it, and retrieved the framed photograph of Trevor. Gently she removed it from its nest of protective bubble wrap.

"Ooooh." Madison sighed appreciatively as she caught sight of what it was. She waved eager, beckoning hands in Mary-Kate's general direction. "Show, then tell all."

"His name is Trevor Reynolds," Mary-Kate said, more than happy to oblige. She went to sit beside Madison, handing her the picture. "Former best friend and current true love."

"Good taste on both counts," Madison commented. She studied Trevor's photograph in silence for a moment. "I know that males don't appreciate female remarks of this nature, but since it's just you and me, I can tell you the truth: He looks nice."

"He *is* nice," Mary-Kate acknowledged. "I think that was what made me fall for him. For the record, he's also funny, smart, has the most beautiful brown eyes in the entire world, and is tops in the kissing department."

"Stop!" Madison cried. She thrust the photo back into Mary-Kate's arms. "You'll make me insanely jealous, and I was just starting to like you!"

"Sorry," Mary-Kate said with a completely unapologetic smile. She scooted off the window seat to place Trevor's photo on the desk by her bed.

"You know what?" Madison suddenly asked. "I'm starving."

"Wow, me, too!" Mary-Kate exclaimed. "I didn't even think about the whole food aspect of the no-dorm thing until right this minute. Guess we'll have to fend for ourselves."

"Fortunately for you, I'm from here, so I know where to shop for the best stuff," Madison replied.

"How about if I do a quick late-night food run while you tackle the rest of your bags?"

"Sounds great to me," Mary-Kate acknowledged. "Want some money?"

"Why don't I shop first, then we can all four settle up," Madison suggested. "That will give us an excuse for a household powwow."

"Okay," Mary-Kate said. "Thanks."

"Don't mention it," Madison said as she slung a black bag across one shoulder. She walked to their bedroom door, then turned back. "Though you realize, of course, that, since I'm doing the first nice roommate-type thing, you will owe me one."

"You sneak!" Mary-Kate cried. She was rewarded by the sound of Madison's departing laughter.

That's exactly the kind of stunt Trevor might have pulled, Mary-Kate thought.

She glanced over at his picture. At the sight of his familiar smiling face, love and longing swarmed through her. On impulse Mary-Kate moved to her own shoulder bag and opened it. She pulled out her cell phone and hit AUTO-DIAL for Trevor's new dorm room. In just a moment she'd hear Trevor's voice. She'd be able to tell him all about the dorm catastrophe and the—

"Hey, you've reached Trevor and Max," a voice Mary-Kate had never heard before said into her ear. Trevor's new roommate had recorded the message.

"That's the good news. The bad news is, we can't take your call right now. But, hey—don't be shy. We really want to hear from you, especially if you're a girl! Talk after the beep."

A quick, high-pitched *beep* made Mary-Kate wince.

"Hi, Trevor, it's Mary-Kate," she said when the annoying sound was over. "We made it. We're here. But it's been quite a day. You'll never guess—the pipes in our dorm exploded! Before we actually got here, I mean. Not in front of our very eyes. We're in temporary quarters across the street at this professor's house. Not that he's actually in it."

Could I sound more lame? I don't think so.

"Anyway," she hurried on, "I just wanted to call and say hi. If you want to call back, use my cell number, okay? We don't have a regular phone yet. Okay, talk to you later. Bye."

Well, that went well, she thought sarcastically as she punched the OFF button. During the few minutes it had taken to unsuccessfully try to reach Trevor, Mary-Kate's good mood had dissolved into glumness. All of a sudden she realized how tired she was. This new college stuff was exciting and great, and Madison was definitely wonderful, but even her cheery roommate couldn't take the place of the one thing Mary-Kate hadn't been able to pack.

Her true love.

Mary***Kate invites AshleyO to Instant Message!

Mary***Kate: Hey, gal upstairs. How's
  it going?

AshleyO: Fine. How else?

Mary***Kate: Happy 2 hear it. Does this
  place rock, or what?

AshleyO: Definitely. But remember . . .

Mary***Kate: I know. I know. Don't
  trash the professor's house.

AshleyO: U talk to Trevor yet?

Mary***Kate: Not yet. Left voice
  message. Madison out for munchies.
  Come down soon.

AshleyO: Will do. Bye 4 now!

CHAPTER SIX

The first official household meeting of the fantastic four is now in session!" Madison declared. "First order of business: refreshments."

With a flourish she plunked a bag of corn chips, a jar of salsa, and several cans of soda onto the kitchen table.

It was pretty late, but the twins were still on California time. After Ashley called their parents to let them know they had arrived safe and sound, Mary-Kate had spent most of the night finishing up unpacking and trying not to stare at her cell phone. To her disappointment and surprise, Trevor hadn't phoned her back yet. *Wouldn't he stop at his dorm room before dinner? Even just to get a meal card or something?*

"Fantastic four," she commented now, forcing her worries to the back of her mind. "I like that. Makes us sound like superheroes or something."

"Precisely why I chose it," Madison said. "We're freshmen. I figure that means we need all the empowerment we can get! Which brings me to the second order of business: paying me back for point number one!"

From their places around the table Mary-Kate, Zoe, and Ashley laughed.

"You all know Madison, don't you?" Mary-Kate said. "She's kind of bossy, but you'll get used to it. I know I have!"

"Uh-oh. Guilty as charged. I admit it," Madison said. "It's an occupational hazard of being the oldest of eight kids."

"So, how *do* we handle the food budget?" Ashley asked. "After we pay Madison back for tonight's treats, I mean."

"I have a suggestion." Zoe spoke up quickly.

"Great. Let's hear it," Mary-Kate said, even as she noticed Ashley's pursed lips.

"I was thinking we could each pitch in a specific amount for stuff we'll all eat. Chips, milk, cereal—things like that. Then, if there are individual items we want, we can pay for them ourselves and label them," Zoe explained. "If we want to plan a big meal together, whoever buys the stuff can save the receipts, just like Madison did. Then we settle up afterward."

"Okay by me," Ashley said quickly, as if eager to agree.

"Me, too," Madison seconded.

"Well, that was easy," Mary-Kate commented.

"Though I hope the dorm gets repaired soon,"

Madison commented. "I must be the only girl on campus looking forward to institutional food! My budget isn't set up for too many extras."

Unlike Mary-Kate, Ashley, and Zoe, who had all come from out of state, Madison was a local. She was already holding down a part-time job at a local coffee bar to help pay her tuition. In addition to taking a regular load of classes, she would have a pretty full schedule.

"Let's settle up for this stuff right now," Mary-Kate said as she popped the top on a can of soda.

Madison produced the receipt and the girls got down to business. Then, at Ashley's suggestion, they made a quick shopping list. More money exchanged hands.

"Well, that's that!" Mary-Kate said. "Now that we have those pesky household decisions out of the way, we can get to the really important stuff."

Ashley cocked an eyebrow in her sister's direction. "Which is?"

"What to wear to the big party at the student union tomorrow night. Can you say *duh*?" Mary-Kate replied with a laugh.

"Duh!" Ashley promptly replied.

"You know," Madison commented, her tone thoughtful, "this house would be a great place to throw a party, too. It's so big."

"I hate to be a killjoy, but the RA warned us about

stuff like that, remember?" Ashley reminded them.

"So we throw a very small, responsible party," Mary-Kate said.

"But—" Ashley protested. She fell silent when Mary-Kate held up a hand.

"*But* we're getting ahead of ourselves here," she said. "Let's stay focused on the event tomorrow. The question remains: What shall we wear? I'm thinking—"

She was interrupted by a noise from the front of the house. One that sounded precisely like a key being turned in the locks on the front door.

"Did you guys hear that?" Mary-Kate asked.

"I seriously hope that's not Professor Donovan," Zoe commented.

The front door closed firmly. Footsteps moved toward the kitchen.

"Hello?" a voice called.

"Back here. In the kitchen," Mary-Kate called back.

Madison's eyes widened. "Wait a minute," she whispered loudly. "That sounded like a . . ."

The footsteps halted as a figure appeared in the doorway.

It was very definitely *not* Professor Donovan. Though it very definitely *was* a guy.

He was tall and sandy-haired, with the sort of lean yet muscular build that, for some reason, always summoned up images of cowboys in Mary-Kate's mind. Though, judging from his backpack and the duffel bag slung over one shoulder, she figured this guy was more likely to be rock climbing than riding the range. His deep blue eyes surveyed the group of four young women staring at him in openmouthed astonishment. He looked a little embarrassed.

"I can't believe it," he finally said, as he dropped the duffel to the floor with a *thump*. "It's happened again."

Mary-Kate was the first to find her voice. "You get assigned to girls' dorms all the time?"

"Nope, but I do get mistaken for one. A girl, I mean."

"In what alternate universe?" Madison blurted out. Then she turned bright red.

At this, the amusement in the newcomer's eyes finally won out. He laughed. "Maybe I should introduce myself," he said. He came into the room, hand extended, and offered it to Madison, who somehow managed to turn an even brighter shade of red while she shook it. "My name is Leslie Davis," he finished.

"Did you say *Leslie*?" Mary-Kate asked.

He turned toward her, hand still extended.

Completely on autopilot, Mary-Kate shook it.

"I can see the light bulb above your head going off," he commented. "Excellent. My parents named me after Leslie Howard, the movie actor."

"The guy who played Ashley in *Gone With the Wind*?" Ashley asked.

"That's right," he said, his tone expressing his surprise.

Mary-Kate saw him blink as he took in the fact that the two of them were twins.

"How come you know that?" he asked. "Not many people our age do."

"*My* name is *Ashley*!" Ashley said with a laugh. "You've already met my sister, Mary-Kate, and her roommate, Madison. This is my roommate, Zoe."

"Pleased to meet you all," Leslie said with a smile. "Well, I hate to greet and run, but I guess I'd better see if I can get a hold of my RA to straighten this out." He rummaged in the duffel and extracted his cell. "Okay if I make the call from the living room?" he asked.

"Sure," Mary-Kate said.

Absolute silence reigned in the kitchen while Leslie made his call. A moment later he reappeared, looking frustrated.

"Uh-oh," Mary-Kate said.

Leslie gave her a somewhat weary smile. "You got that right. My RA says he's going to have to get back to me tomorrow about temporary housing. Apparently he thinks I'd be delighted to hang out on the streets for the night—with all my gear, of course."

"There's no reason for you to do that," Madison

said suddenly. She cast a quick look around the table as if seeking support. "There's actually plenty of room here. Doesn't that sofa in the den pull out?"

"That's right. It does," Mary-Kate put in. "There's no reason Leslie couldn't stay in that room, is there?"

"As long as we establish a few basic household rules—along the lines of not walking around in our underwear," Ashley said with a twinkle in her eye, "I don't see why not. This is just a temporary situation for us all anyhow."

"If you really wouldn't mind, that would be great," Leslie acknowledged, relief in his voice. "I can concentrate on making sure I get my classes lined up first, then sort out the living arrangements."

"It's settled then," Zoe said decisively. She stood up. "Why don't I show you where the den is?"

"Great," Leslie said again. "Thanks." He gave a smile that managed to encompass them all, then followed Zoe, re-hoisting his duffel on his way out the door.

"I hope we did the right thing," Ashley said, slightly worried. "It's a *little* unusual."

"Of course it's the right thing!" Madison protested. "We're being Good Samaritans. Not only that, he's incredibly cute. How lucky can four college girls get?"

Madison_Ave invites Mary***Kate to Instant Message!

Madison_Ave: Hey, u. Our first IM as
    roomies. Can u dig it?
Mary***Kate: Absolutely! :-D U were
    gone when I got up this morning.
    Where are u?
Madison_Ave: Came over 2 work 2 get
    next week's schedule. I'm on my way
    back now. I'll meet u at the book-
    store. Important question. Cannot
    delay. Is Leslie hot, or what?
Mary***Kate: Oh, yeah. U interested?
Madison_Ave: Maybe. Actually, I thought
    he sort of noticed u.
Mary***Kate: It's just the twin thing.
    Happens all the time.
Madison_Ave: OK, if u say so. U think I
    did the right thing asking him 2
    stay?
Mary***Kate: Absolutely! UR the best!
Madison_Ave: Well, sure. That's what
    they all say.
Mary***Kate: Not 2 mention modest.
Madison_Ave: C U soon.

CHAPTER SEVEN

*I*f this is a sample of the social life at Lawton, I am definitely going to like it here, Ashley thought.

The Welcome, New Students party at the campus student union was in full swing. For the last hour or so the townhouse group, including Leslie, had been making the scene. They'd managed to stick together at first, but the growing crowd had soon made that impossible.

Currently Ashley was on her own, a situation she might have found overwhelming. But this time, it was just plain enjoyable to be with lots of other people having fun, even if she didn't know most of them. Not only that, the party was a great place to people-watch.

Take that guy over in the corner, Ashley thought.

In her lifetime of guy-watching experiences, he was one of the best-looking boys Ashley had ever seen. And, of course, he was surrounded by a crowd of adoring females. Though his looks had been the first thing to grab her attention, the way he handled himself was what kept Ashley focused on him. He seemed completely natural and unself-conscious, content to let others do most of the talking. That alone made him unusual. In Ashley's experience, anyone who attracted that much attention usually made sure he or she kept it by some kind of showing off.

I wonder who he is, Ashley thought. *We're all new here, so there's no time like the present to find out!* Slowly she worked her way through the crowd toward him.

What's wrong with me? Mary-Kate wondered.

Here she was at her first official college party, surrounded by people who were having a good time. *She'd* been having a good time, at least at the start. But not long after being separated from the rest of her new friends, Mary-Kate had been startled to discover that her fun was steadily declining.

It didn't take her too long to identify the cause.

Trevor. Or, more specifically, the lack of Trevor. Instinctively Mary-Kate kept turning to share things with him, as if expecting to find him at her side. It made her chuckle at herself at first. But the joke definitely wore thin as the evening went on. Mary-Kate had expected to miss Trevor in the quiet moments, the ones when she was all alone. But she'd never expected to miss him so keenly in a roomful of people.

Why hasn't he called?

Over an entire day had now gone by, and Trevor still hadn't been in touch. Could their long-distance relationship be failing already? Could it be over before it even had the chance to start?

"Could you try not getting carried away for once in your life?" Mary-Kate muttered to herself.

"What?" said a voice at her side.

Startled, Mary-Kate whirled to find her house-mate, Leslie, standing beside her. She'd been so engrossed in her own thoughts, she hadn't noticed him approach her.

"Hey," he said. "How's it going?" Then, before Mary-Kate could answer, he leaned in close so he didn't have to shout, his dark blue eyes searching her face. "You okay?" he asked. "You look sort of—I don't know."

"Bummed," Mary-Kate supplied, somewhat to her own surprise. There was just something about Leslie that made her want to move closer, to confide. Of course it didn't hurt that Madison was right: The guy was gorgeous, no two ways about it.

"The truth is, I'm missing my boyfriend. He's three thousand miles away in California."

"Doing the long-distance thing, huh?" Leslie asked sympathetically. "That's tough."

"I called as soon as I got in, and I haven't heard back," Mary-Kate blurted out. "I don't know what that means. Should I be worried? Should I let it go?"

"Guys don't have the same time frame about phone calls that girls have," Leslie said. "It doesn't mean anything at all. Maybe his roommate just forgot to give him the message."

"You're right. I know you're right," Mary-Kate said. "I don't know why I'm getting so freaked."

"Well, hey, if you really like the guy . . ." Leslie began. At precisely that moment, Mary-Kate's cell phone gave its melodic trill. "There! You see?" Leslie said. "I'll bet that's him."

"If it is, I'll buy you dinner," Mary-Kate promised. Swiftly she got out her cell. "Nope," she said after studying the screen for a moment. "It's Ashley. She's sending me an IM."

Hot new guy sighting, Ashley's message said. *Must have scoop. Where R U? I need help!*

"Looks like sisterly duty calls," Mary-Kate commented, her good humor almost restored. "Thanks for taking the time to listen, Leslie. I really appreciate it."

For a split second Leslie's blue eyes were intent on Mary-Kate's face. Mary-Kate felt a finger of some emotion she couldn't quite name creep up her spine. Then Leslie smiled and the moment passed.

"What are housemates for?" he asked. "See you later."

"Okay," Mary-Kate said.

Then, messaging for Ashley to meet her over by an enormous potted palm, Mary-Kate set off to render sibling assistance.

• • •

"Well, did you get close to him? Who is he?" Ashley inquired breathlessly as soon as Mary-Kate returned from some fact-finding.

"Down, girl!" Mary-Kate said with a laugh. "His name is Dave Calhoun, and he's from New Mexico." She folded her arms triumphantly across her chest.

A spasm of disbelief crossed Ashley's face. "That's it?"

"What do you mean, *that's it*? I was lucky to get that much!" Mary-Kate protested. "Getting close to that guy is like trying to cozy up to a rock star. He's surrounded by adoring fans."

"You had to have found out *something* else," Ashley wailed.

"Well, he's also into anything outdoors. But you can tell that just by looking at him."

"Who are we just looking at?" Madison's voice suddenly cut in. "Also, where is he, and on whose behalf am I checking him out?"

"Dave Calhoun. Ashley. Over there," Mary-Kate said as she turned to point discreetly. "Not necessarily in that order."

Madison turned in the direction Mary-Kate had indicated. "Wow, great choice, Ashley," she said as she turned back. "What's the plan?"

"I haven't gotten that far yet," Ashley admitted. "I'm still in the information-gathering stage." She made a face at Mary-Kate.

"Hey, I told you," Mary-Kate said. "I did my best."

"There you guys are! You are *not* going to believe this," Zoe said, finding the threesome. "I just asked the cutest guy to our party—and he said yes!"

"What guy?" Madison inquired.

"Party? What party?" Ashley asked.

"I spotted this incredibly hot guy right after we got here," Zoe explained. "But it took all night to get close to him! I knew I had to say something memorable, so I invited him to the party we talked about throwing. It's tomorrow night, by the way."

"That's a great idea!" Mary-Kate said.

"As long as it's a small one," Ashley said. "I hate to sound like the den mother, but you remember what our RA said."

"Well, of course I do," Zoe said, sounding ever so slightly miffed. "What's the matter? Don't you trust me?"

"Of course I do," Ashley said. "It's just—"

"So, what's this hottie's name?" Madison broke in, as if determined to head off trouble.

"Dave," Zoe said. "He's from New Mexico, and . . ."

"Really into anything outdoors," Mary-Kate finished. "I can't believe this!"

"This is terrible. It has all the makings of a disaster!" Madison said dramatically.

"What on earth are you talking about?" Zoe demanded.

"*I* spotted Dave-from-New-Mexico, too," Ashley

said as calmly as she could. *Just what I don't need,* she thought. *Something else Zoe staked a claim to first!*

"This is really bad news," Madison said again, adopting a gloomy tone.

"For crying out loud," Zoe said. "All I did was ask him to our party. That seems pretty innocent to me."

"Don't you see? That's just how conflicts start," Madison insisted. "I saw this movie once, *The Same Guy*, where two best friends went after the same boy. They figured out he wasn't worth it in the end, but in the meantime the friendship was completely destroyed! We can't let that happen to any of us."

"How about a pact?" Mary-Kate suggested. "No dating the same guy. No even trying. All in favor say 'aye.' *Aye!*"

"Aye," Madison said at once.

"Aye," Zoe put in quickly.

"Aye," Ashley said with a mental sigh. *So much for the cutest guy in the room.* "Though Zoe and I both want big cosmic brownie points for agreeing to give up Dave."

"Absolutely," Zoe said with what Ashley hoped was a grateful smile.

"Now that that's settled," Ashley said, "let's talk about this party we've just decided to throw!"

"Hello?" Mary-Kate said eagerly into her cell phone later that night.

The rest of the household had long since gone to bed. But Mary-Kate was too keyed up to sleep. Why hadn't Trevor called? Not even the late-night movie on TV could take her mind off the question. She'd run into the kitchen to avoid awakening Madison as soon as her cell rang.

"Hey!"

"Trevor!" she said joyfully. "You sound great. Hi."

"Hi, yourself," said his familiar voice. "How's life on the East Coast?"

"Good," Mary-Kate replied. *Though not as good as it would be if you were here.* "Did you get my message? The one about the dorm catastrophe?"

"Sort of," Trevor answered with a chuckle. "Max erased it, then forgot to tell me you'd called. I only found out a couple of minutes ago. He's kind of spacey sometimes. I think he actually registered for some absentminded-artist-in-training courses."

"That's okay," Mary-Kate said as relief at the simple explanation flooded through her.

"So, here I was, all lonesome and figuring you'd forgotten all about me. . . ."

"And I was thinking you'd forgotten all about me!" Mary-Kate finished.

It's okay. We're still on the same wavelength, she thought. She tucked her feet under her and settled in for the call, happy just to listen to Trevor's voice.

Mary***Kate invites AshleyO to Instant Message!

Mary***Kate: Trevor called!

AshleyO: Gr8t news! How r things in the land of true love?

Mary***Kate: Happily ever after, thank you very much! I didn't want to wake you, but I kept hearing thumping up there . . . ?

AshleyO: That would be Zoe's music on the stereo. She's a retro-music freak. Who knew? Current idol: Hendrix.

Mary***Kate: Yikes! That's heavy-duty.

AshleyO: Tell me about it! Must add earplugs to shopping list for tomorrow! Help me remember.

Mary***Kate: You got it!

CHAPTER EIGHT

I still think we ought to have crepe paper," Zoe said. "And maybe some balloons we could blow up and stick on the walls. You know, sort of a sock-hop approach."

"I like it. I honestly do," Ashley said. "It's just, I'm concerned about sticking things up on the walls. The RA said . . ."

"I *know* what the RA said," Zoe said with a roll of her eyes. "It's all you've been talking about for the last half hour!"

The four roommates were standing in the party decorations section of Shop Mart, a nearby every-thing-in-one store. They'd already taken care of the easy stuff—the party food. The decorations were turn-ing out to be more of a challenge.

Much as Ashley appreciated Zoe's creative ideas, and she genuinely did, she also had what she consid-ered to be legitimate concerns about them. They couldn't go around thumbtacking and taping things to the walls of the professor's townhouse.

"Down, girl!" Madison said with a laugh as she gave Zoe a light sock on the arm. "No fighting over party planning. It's simply not allowed."

"For the record," Mary-Kate put in, "I think Ashley's right. The concept is great, Zoe, but we've got to be careful in Professor Donovan's house. Maybe we could put balloons and streamers around the food instead."

"That sounds good," Ashley said quickly.

"Okay," Zoe said, sounding slightly sulky. "If that's what you want."

"I'm trying to give *you* what *you* want!" Ashley said. She felt her temper start to slip. She'd been fighting to hold on to it all morning, a thing made more difficult by the fact that Zoe's music had kept her up the previous night.

"What else is on our list?" Madison asked quickly.

"Earth to Madison," Mary-Kate said. "*You*'ve got the list!"

Madison slapped her forehead. "Oh, right." She did a quick consult. "Believe it or not, I think we're done. Though Zoe did want to look at posters. For your actual dorm room, that is."

"That's right!" Zoe said, her tone brightening. She set off down the aisle at once.

"Looking for anything in particular?" Mary-Kate asked as they walked along.

"Optical illusions," Zoe said.

"What?" Ashley cried.

"You know, those big optical illusions posters," Zoe explained. "Or maybe sixties pop art. Something bright with a lot of energy." They reached the picture frames aisle, which included a large selection of posters. Zoe flipped through them quickly, then stepped back to reveal two, holding them up side by side.

"Perfect!" she said.

Ashley looked at Zoe's selections. The first was an enormous black and white spiral that made her feel as if she were being sucked straight into its middle. Beside it was a poster of a list of colors, spelled out in colors other than what the words themselves meant. *Green* appeared in blue. *Red* was spelled out in purple. *Yellow* was orange.

At least it will be a total-body experience, Ashley thought. Her head and stomach would hurt at the same time!

"Aren't these fantastic?" Zoe said. She gave Ashley a bright smile.

Ashley opened her mouth to say she actually preferred Mary-Kate's collection of Ansel Adams posters, but to her shock she heard herself say, "Absolutely." For one split second she thought she saw surprise flicker across Zoe's features. But the expression came and went so quickly, Ashley figured she'd only imagined it.

"Excellent," Zoe said. She located the rolled

posters in the bin and pulled them out. "Okay, I guess we're done. Let's check out, go home, and get ready for the party!"

"I am definitely with you," Madison declared. She pushed the laden shopping cart briskly down the aisle, Zoe at her side. Ashley moved as if to follow, but Mary-Kate held her back with a firm hand on her arm.

"Ashley Olsen," she hissed. "You hate stuff like that! Why didn't you say something? You're letting her walk all over you!"

"I am not," Ashley said. "It's just . . . we haven't hit it off as easily as you and Madison have. I figured I could compromise."

"You're doing more than compromising. You're turning into a doormat!" Mary-Kate declared. "You already let her pick out everything else about the room. Why couldn't *she* compromise this time?"

"I didn't *let* her pick everything out, Mary-Kate," Ashley said, growing testy. "She'd done it before I even got here! I'm just trying to create a good roommate relationship."

"Okay," Mary-Kate said, still sounding doubtful. "Just be careful, Ash. There's a fine line between creating a great roommate and creating a monster!"

Madison_Ave invites Mary★★★Kate to Instant Message!

Madison_Ave: OK. What gives with the
    vibe between Ashley and Zoe?
Mary★★★Kate: Wish I knew. Working on
    it.
Madison_Ave: Anything I can do, let me
    know.
Mary★★★Kate: Will do. Thanks. C U B4
    the party!

CHAPTER NINE

O
kay, I have to admit it," Ashley said as she stood at the dining room table and surveyed the houseful of people all having a good time. "Throwing a party was an excellent idea. Just so long as it doesn't get any bigger than this!"

From her position beside Ashley, where she'd been replenishing the chips and dip, Mary-Kate gave a laugh. "You're the only person I know who can say *thank you* and *no, thank you* at the same time," she remarked.

"Unfair!" Ashley protested. "I'm just trying to keep things in perspective."

"That's okay," Mary-Kate said, giving her sister's shoulder a comforting pat. "I know you can't help it. It's a character flaw."

"You have a flaw?" Leslie suddenly inquired as he materialized at Mary-Kate's side. He examined her face. "Where?"

Mary-Kate gave him a playful shove. "Not me, you dope. Her." She pointed at her sister.

"Thanks a lot!" Ashley cried.

Leslie turned toward Ashley and gave her a quick wink. "Sorry. Still can't see it," he said.

"That's because you're not looking hard enough," Mary-Kate teased.

"Go make yourself useful," Ashley told her sister as the doorbell rang.

Laughing, Mary-Kate moved to answer it. Ashley couldn't help but notice the way Leslie's gaze followed Mary-Kate across the room.

"She seems . . . happier," he commented.

"Her boyfriend, Trevor, phoned last night," Ashley said. "You were right. His roommate forgot to give him the message."

"I figured it was something like that," Leslie said.

"Mary-Kate told me how supportive you were," Ashley went on. "And also how much she appreciated it."

The quick smile Leslie gave didn't quite reach his eyes. "All in a day's work for a housemate, right?" he asked.

Before Ashley could respond, he gave a quick wave, touched her arm lightly in farewell, and moved to join an acquaintance across the room. The doorbell rang once more. Before one of the housemates could answer it, the door opened, and another group of students surged in. *We didn't invite this many people, did we?* Ashley thought. *We don't even know this many people yet!* The house was getting so packed, she couldn't see from one room to the next. And the noise level was rising right along with the body count.

Ashley returned to the kitchen to check on the food supplies. The kitchen was long and narrow, with a cozy eating nook at the far end. Ashley could barely see it through the crowd. Slowly she made her way down the kitchen's length, smiling and stopping to chat as she went. She wanted to have a good time at her own party, after all! When she'd almost reached the eating nook, she stopped short.

Zoe and Dave were its most conspicuous occupants, sitting side by side. Dave's expression was animated as he told the small group a story. Zoe kept her gaze fixed on his face, as if the rest of the world simply didn't exist. Ashley edged a little closer. Dave was describing a long pass. *They're talking about football? Zoe isn't interested in football, is she?*

Ashley felt a slow burn of frustration start in the pit of her stomach. She'd been trying so hard to get along with Zoe. She'd even made a pact to ignore her attraction to the first interesting guy she'd seen in ages. A pact Zoe had readily agreed to. But here Zoe was, monopolizing Dave Calhoun as if the agreement they'd made wasn't important at all.

I guess Mary-Kate was right, Ashley thought. *I should have stood up for myself before now.* A party was hardly the place to start, though. She should avoid letting Zoe see that she was miffed. Turning around, Ashley began to make her way back out of the kitchen. She'd just reached the dining room when she heard yelling from the front doorway.

"The noise level over here is completely unacceptable!" she heard the voice shout over the crowd. "If you don't keep it down, I'll call the campus police!"

Oh, no! Ashley thought. She hurried forward as quickly as the crush of partying bodies would allow. She was halfway across the living room when she spotted Mary-Kate, who had a death grip on the partially open front door. She was face-to-face with the guy from next door, the young professor trying to get tenure!

"I'm sorry," Mary-Kate was saying. "I didn't realize—"

The young professor cut her off. "I need peace and quiet to do my work. I thought I made that clear the first time."

"First time?" Mary-Kate echoed just as Ashley reached her side. "I'm sorry, have we met before?"

"*We* met, the day we moved in," Ashley said swiftly, relieved to hear somebody in the room behind her turn down the stereo. "And you did make it clear. I don't think any of us realized we'd gotten so loud. I apologize for the inconvenience."

"Yes, well . . ."

Ashley watched as the professor's gaze traveled between her and Mary-Kate. *He probably thinks we did it on purpose, just to bother him,* she thought.

"Just so long as it doesn't happen again," he grumbled.

"It won't. We'll see to it," Ashley promised.

"All right, then," the professor said. For a moment Ashley thought he'd say something more. Instead, he turned abruptly on one heel and marched down the front walk.

"Whew!" Mary-Kate breathed as she closed the door behind him. "Who *was* that guy?"

"The professor who lives next door. I don't know his name," Ashley answered. "And I'm not so sure I want him to know ours!"

"Whatever his name is, he sure knows how to kill a good party," Mary-Kate said. "Guess we'd better see about wrapping this up. I'll go find Madison."

"And I'll find Leslie," Ashley said. She didn't have to look for Zoe. She already knew where she was.

"That went well, don't you think?" Madison asked several hours later. She and Mary-Kate were flopped on the beds in their room, hashing over the events of the evening.

"Absolutely," Mary-Kate said. "If you don't count the very end, of course."

"I sure hope I never get that guy for a class!" Madison exclaimed. "Who is he, anyhow?"

"Beats me," Mary-Kate said with a shrug. "So, spot anyone you want to hang out with? Besides me, of course."

Madison's eyes were dancing with laughter as she answered. "Well, there *were* one or two guys. . . ."

•   •   •

Ashley could hear a wild guitar riff even through the closed bathroom door. She turned the water off, her nightly face ritual complete, and the sound got even louder. If they weren't careful, she thought, the next-door neighbor would be back—this time to complain about Zoe's stereo!

She opened the bathroom door, snapped off the light, and walked across the hall. Zoe was sitting on her bed with her back propped against the wall as she flipped through a magazine. She didn't look up when Ashley came into the room.

"I really hate to mention this," Ashley said, "but I think we should consider turning the stereo down."

"If you say so," Zoe replied.

Ashley turned the sound down several notches. "So," she said as she went to sit on her own bed, "did you have a good time at the party?"

"The best," Zoe said, looking up at last. "Dave Calhoun told me the funniest story."

"I didn't know you were a football fan," Ashley said.

"How did you know it was about football?" Zoe asked. "Oh, wait a minute. I get it. You were spying on us."

"I wasn't *spying*," Ashley said. "I came into the kitchen and saw you two together. We did make a pact, Zoe."

Zoe punched the pillow she had stuffed behind

her back, her expression sullen. "Dave was our guest, Ashley. I invited him myself. What did you want me to do, blow him off?"

"Of course not—" Ashley began.

"Good," Zoe interrupted. "At least we agree on something." She climbed off the bed, crossed the room, and turned the stereo back up. Then she turned off her nightstand lamp, plunging her side of the room into darkness. "I'd like to get some sleep now, if you don't mind."

Good luck! Ashley thought, turning off her own lamp. At the rate things were going, she wouldn't get a decent night's sleep till she went home at Thanksgiving!

Why, when she was so determined for things to go right, did everything between her and Zoe keep turning out so wrong?

Mary★★★Kate invites Trevor86 to Instant Message!

Trevor86 is unavailable at this time.

AshleyO invites Felicity_girl to Instant Message!

AshleyO: Hey, girlfriend. U still up?

Felicity_girl: Absolutely. Remember
  it's 3 hours earlier here.

AshleyO: Right. I knew that.

Felicity_girl: So, what's up?

AshleyO: Nothing, really. Just wanted 2
  hear a friendly voice.

Felicity_girl: Uh-oh. Got roommate
  troubles, huh?

AshleyO: Guilty as charged.

Felicity_girl: Incroyable! New French
  vocabulary word. It means, I can't
  believe it! Whoever that girl is,
  she must be nuts!

AshleyO: I don't think it's that! But I
  just can't figure her out.

Felicity_girl: Hang in there, pal.
  Maybe she's just doing the first-
  time-away-from-home freak thing.

AshleyO: I'll remember that. Good
  thought.

CHAPTER TEN

Ashley was up bright and early the next morning. Sunshine streamed in through the bedroom window. There was nothing like a beautiful new day for a clean, fresh start. Not only that, she'd also be participating in her first orientation-week activity: a walking tour of the campus and the surrounding area.

Even the state of the townhouse as she made her way to the kitchen didn't dim Ashley's good mood, though she had to admit they had come pretty close to breaking the rules about not trashing the professor's house. The damage was all superficial, though—nothing a good cleaning wouldn't fix in no time. Ashley decided to start in the kitchen, where she'd already put the teakettle on to boil. She'd do as much as she could, then leave the rest for her roommates. She was only one of five, after all.

Opening the cupboard beneath the sink, she extracted a large black trash bag and began to fill it with party debris. By the time the teakettle whistled cheerfully, she was almost done.

If only you could tidy up relationships as easily as you can paper plates, she thought as she opened the fridge to rummage for some breakfast. *Score! English muffins.* She was just about to take one when she noticed a name in big block letters across the top: ZOE. *So much for that breakfast plan,* Ashley thought. She'd just finished stuffing the muffin back into the bag when Zoe came into the kitchen. Talk about the nick of time!

"This house is a complete disaster," Zoe said tiredly. "Why didn't I notice that last night?"

Ashley gave a chuckle. "Easy," she said. "We were all having too much fun." All of a sudden she realized she still had the open bag of English muffins in one hand. "I wasn't going to take one," she said quickly. "I got them out before I realized they were yours."

"That's okay," Zoe said. She gave a huge yawn, walked to the eating nook, and sat down. "You can have one if you want."

"Really?" Ashley asked. "That would be great. They're my favorite."

"Mine, too," Zoe said. "Pop one in for me?"

"Sure." *See? We can do this,* Ashley thought excitedly as she slipped two English muffins into the four-slice toaster. "I made tea," she said. "You want some?"

"Sure, thanks," Zoe said.

Ashley poured a mug and placed it beside her.

"I was wondering if I could ask you for a favor," Zoe said, her fingers tracing the rim of the mug.

Ashley was so surprised, she completely ignored the English muffins as they shot up in the toaster.

"Sure," she said. "What?"

"I need to check in with my parents," Zoe said. She made a face. "Or at least with my mom. But I don't have a cell phone. I wanted one, but my dad . . . he said college was already costing him enough. I know I could go to a pay phone, but—"

"Don't be silly," Ashley said at once. "You can use my cell. I'm going on that walking tour this morning anyway. I'll leave the phone on my desk before I go."

"Thanks. I really appreciate it," Zoe said. She pulled in a breath. "Ashley, I—"

"How can you two possibly be up so early?" Mary-Kate's voice interrupted. "Don't you know it's against the law?"

"In which case, you're as busted as we are!" Ashley informed her. "Omigosh!" she exclaimed as she caught sight of the kitchen clock. Swiftly she snatched a muffin from the toaster, buttered it, and wrapped it in a napkin. "I've got to dash, or I'll be late. Thanks for the English muffin, Zoe."

"Sure," Zoe said.

"Oh, boy," Ashley heard Mary-Kate say as she dashed for the stairs. "I love English muffins."

"It's Ashley, right?"

At the sound of her name, Ashley turned from

studying the map the tour leader had just passed out. *Uh-oh,* she thought even as her heart gave a little leap.

"Guilty as charged," she said. "And you're Dave, right?"

"Right. So, this is great," he said. "You're going on the walk?"

"Absolutely." Ashley nodded. "I figured, you know, any chance to be outside until classes start."

"My thought exactly," Dave Calhoun said with a smile. He fell into step beside her as the group started off. Ashley felt a twinge of guilt, then quickly fought it down. She hadn't encouraged Dave at all. If he wanted to walk beside her, that was his decision, and who was she to fight it?

"Great party you guys threw last night," Dave said as they ambled along. "Kind of a shame about the way it ended, though."

"I couldn't agree more," Ashley said. "Our next-door neighbor definitely has noise issues."

"I hear that," Dave said.

"So did he. That was the problem!"

Dave gave her a slow smile. *Oh, wow,* Ashley thought. *He is absolutely gorgeous when he does that.* Not as if it was painful to look at him the rest of the time! Up close his eyes were a really unusual color, a sort of stormy gray.

"So, you're from New Mexico, right?" Ashley asked as the group meandered across the campus.

"Yup," Dave said. "From Taos. What about you?"

"Southern California," Ashley said. She was rewarded once again with his smile.

"Surfer girl, huh?"

"Among other talents," Ashley acknowledged.

"I've always wanted to learn to surf," Dave said. "It's one sport I've never done. Hey, listen. I'm getting an idea. There's a great little burger joint over on B Street."

She'd heard about that area of town. The espresso bar where Madison worked was nearby.

"I was thinking I'd head over there tonight for a bite. Why don't you come along? You can tell me about your surfing adventures."

Ashley hesitated for about two-tenths of a second. This is *not* a date, she told herself. *Zoe can't mind.* Dave's invitation was simply a result of the casual conversation they'd been having. The get-together this evening would be a continuation of that, nothing more.

"I'd love to," she said. "What time?"

"I might have to get back to you on that," Dave acknowledged. "I have some sports registrations to do this afternoon and I'm not sure what time it will wrap up. Can I call you?"

"Sure," Ashley said. Dave fished a notebook from the pack on his back and Ashley supplied her cell number.

"This will be so excellent," Dave said as he wrote

it down. He stayed by her side for the rest of the trip, and Ashley could feel her heart beating. Somehow, she didn't think it was from the brisk pace of the walk.

"You're awfully good at that. It sort of has me worried," Mary-Kate shouted over the vacuum cleaner's roar.

From his position across the living room, Leslie grinned, then switched off the machine.

"What did you say?" he asked loudly. When he realized what he'd done, he laughed. "Sorry," he said, gesturing toward the vacuum. "I couldn't really hear you before."

"I was just wondering how come you're so good at this cleaning stuff," Mary-Kate replied. *Not to mention how you got to be so cute and what on earth I'm going to do about the fact that I keep noticing it,* she thought.

"Self-defense," Leslie said as he leaned on the vacuum's handle, his blue eyes sparkling. "I come from a family of six kids—three girls and three boys. Every single one of us learned the fine arts of housekeeping and doing laundry. Also mowing the lawn and washing the car."

"Impressive," Mary-Kate commented.

"What can I tell you?" Leslie said with a laugh. "I'm an impressive guy."

"Not to mention modest."

"That goes without saying."

"In that case," Mary-Kate said as she tossed him a rag and a can of spray polish. "Let's see how good you are at dusting."

"That sounds great!"

Ashley heard Zoe's excited voice float down the stairs as she climbed them a couple of hours later. After the walk and a tour of the campus library, Ashley had wandered to the area around B Street, checking out the restaurant where she was going to meet Dave later. It was *not* a date, but that didn't mean Ashley couldn't be prepared.

"Breakfast is my favorite meal of the day," Zoe went on, as Ashley reached the landing. "Where did you say this place was?"

She's making a date! This is fabulous! Ashley thought. She hesitated on the landing, uncertain about whether to go forward or back. She didn't want to eavesdrop, but she didn't want to interrupt Zoe's private conversation either.

"B Street," Zoe said. "Yeah, I know it. My housemate, Madison, works at the Java Connection."

B Street. That sounds familiar, Ashley thought. All of a sudden a horrible suspicion crossed her mind. Ashley had given Dave her cell-phone number, but Zoe had the cell phone!

"You did not!" Zoe said with a quick laugh as her conversation continued. "I happen to know for a fact that nobody can throw a pass that far. I looked it up in the *Guinness Book of World Records* just this morning."

Okay, that does it, Ashley thought. All the evidence pointed squarely to the fact that Zoe was talking to Dave. Not only that, but she was arranging to meet him using Ashley's cell phone! Going back downstairs was no longer an option. Ashley marched toward the bedroom door and pushed it all the way open.

"Oh, hey," Zoe said, when she spotted Ashley. "Here's Ashley now. Great idea about breakfast. I'll see you tomorrow morning. It's for you," she said to Ashley as she held out the phone.

Ashley struggled to keep her expression even as she took the cell. "Hello?"

"Hey, Ashley, it's Dave," he said. "I'm calling about a time for tonight. How does seven o'clock sound?"

"Okay by me," Ashley said.

"Great," Dave said. "See you then."

Without further ado he rang off. Ashley punched the OFF button, then stowed her cell phone in her shoulder bag.

"I know what you must be thinking, but it isn't like that," Ashley said as she turned to Zoe. "I did *not* break our pact."

"You don't know me well enough to know what I'm thinking," Zoe shot back. "And for the record, neither did I. Getting together just sort of came up in conversation when Dave called *you.*"

"That's exactly how *our* meeting plan happened, too," Ashley said quickly. "Spontaneously, during the walking tour. But he needed to call me to confirm the time. Do you always answer other people's phones?"

"My parents weren't home when I called so I had to leave a message," Zoe answered, two bright spots of color appearing on her cheeks. "Your number was the only one I could give them. I thought it was them when the phone rang, so I picked up. Naturally, when I found out it was Dave—"

"You couldn't just blow him off," Ashley interrupted, using Zoe's words of the night before.

"Precisely," Zoe said. "And I don't see why you have to get all bent out of shape about it."

"Would you like me to explain it to you?" Ashley replied.

"Hey," Mary-Kate said suddenly after appearing in the doorway. "What's going on?"

"Nothing," Ashley and Zoe said, in perfect unison.

Mary-Kate rolled her eyes. "Does this *nothing* have to do with Dave-from-New-Mexico?"

"Absolutely," Zoe said.

"Absolutely not," Ashley answered at precisely the same time.

"All right, that does it," Mary-Kate said. Moving into the room, she took Ashley's arm in one hand and Zoe's in the other. "We're going downstairs to hash this out right now, you two. Come on, let's go."

Mary***Kate invites Madison_Ave to Instant Message!

Mary***Kate: Emergency housemate session.
    Living room. Now!
Madison_Ave: On my way home right now.
    Please tell me this has nothing 2 do
    with Dave-from-New Mexico?! :-0
Mary***Kate: Wish I could.
Madison_Ave: Oh, no! :(

CHAPTER ELEVEN

I can't believe you let this happen," Madison wailed several moments later. The entire household, including Leslie, was now assembled in the living room. "I warned you. It's just like in that movie I saw. Before long you'll start saying things you'll both regret. Then you'll never be able to repair your friendship."

How can you repair something you're not even sure exists? Ashley thought, though she kept it to herself.

"I think we need a guy's perspective," Mary-Kate put in, turning to Leslie. "What do think about Dave-from-New-Mexico asking both Ashley and Zoe out?"

"He didn't ask me out," Ashley said at once. "We're not going on a date. The terms *date* and *go out* never even came up."

"Same here," Zoe insisted. "And his last name is Calhoun."

"Calhoun. Great!" Mary-Kate exclaimed, throwing up her hands. "That helps so much."

"Speaking from a guy's perspective," Leslie said, his

voice overriding everyone else's, "what's the problem?"

Mary-Kate shut her mouth with a snap.

"We're all in a new situation here," Leslie went on. "We're all going to be meeting new people. Maybe Dave Calhoun simply prefers to do his meeting one-on-one. Whether or not they're actual dates is up to Ashley and Zoe—and Dave—to determine."

Zoe spoke up. "I have no problem with that."

"Neither do I," Ashley said stoutly.

"Then what's all the fuss about?" Leslie asked. "If you both want to see Dave, you both should go for it. Find out what he's thinking."

"Just so long as nobody rents *The Same Guy*," Madison said with a sigh.

CAMPUS FILM FESTIVAL BEGINS TONIGHT! the poster in the student union declared. SEE OLD CLASSICS. MEET NEW FRIENDS.

What a great idea, Mary-Kate thought. She loved film festivals, and having something to look forward to that night would definitely come in handy.

It was late that afternoon, and, while the situation between Ashley and Zoe had been resolved for the moment, the atmosphere around the townhouse had remained tense. Shortly after lunchtime Madison had jetted off to work and Leslie had attempted a meeting with his new RA.

Taking her cue from Ashley, Mary-Kate had decided

to do a quick test run through the campus, plotting out the path the classes she hoped to take would send her on each day. She soon discovered that she'd be in for a certain amount of aerobic activity—all the class-rooms seemed to be in opposite directions!

On her way back to the townhouse she'd stopped in at the student union for a soda. That was how she'd discovered the poster advertising the film festival. Not only that, but *Breakfast at Tiffany's*, her all-time favorite, was playing that very night! On impulse, Mary-Kate pulled her cell phone out of her bag and punched in Leslie's number.

They had so much in common, *Breakfast at Tiffany's* just had to be a favorite of his, too. In the unlikely event he hadn't seen it yet, she could introduce him to it, a thing that would also be good. Honestly, there was no way to lose!

"Hi, this is Leslie," his voice said into her ear. "If you're hearing this, I'm either talking already or can't talk at all, but *you* can talk when you hear the beep."

Darn! Mary-Kate thought. Leslie must still be meeting with his R.A. *Oh, well, there's still plenty of time. Maybe I can catch him if I run home right now. . . .*

"So," Ashley said. "How did a guy from New Mexico end up on a college campus in New England?"

"The same way you did," Dave said. "I applied."

Ashley gave a startled laugh, but she quickly turned

it into a cough when she realized Dave wasn't being funny. Not intentionally, anyhow.

"Well, it obviously worked," she said. She took a bite of her burger, happy that it gave her mouth something to do besides talk.

It was difficult for her to pinpoint exactly when the evening had begun to go wrong. Dave had been waiting for her in front of the burger place, right on time. And the restaurant itself was unexpectedly charming. Not a retro-fifties diner but the real thing, family owned and operated since its opening. The menus declared that fact proudly.

Ashley had been so delighted, she'd recklessly broken all her usual fat-content-per-occasion rules and ordered both fries *and* a shake. Mint chocolate chip, from homemade ice cream. *Talk about heaven!*

"But if you want to know why I chose Lawton . . ." Dave suddenly went on. He stopped to take a quick slurp of his chocolate malt. "Growing up, I spent the summers here in New York. My aunt—my mom's sister—lives here. It was just the two of them when they were kids, so they're pretty close. I've always liked New England. It's so different from where I grew up. It's so . . . green."

Ashley smiled and nodded. "Compared to the desert, you mean."

Dave smiled, too. "Lawton's sports department is a little smaller than I might have liked," he went on, "but there's still a lot to do, including all the winter sports. I pretty much always knew this was where I wanted to go. I've been here all summer, actually, helping out my aunt. My uncle died last year, so she's on her own."

"That's incredibly nice of you," Ashley commented.

Actually, she decided as she took another bite of burger, the problem wasn't that Dave wasn't an incredibly nice guy. He was. The trouble was that he also had a one-track mind, and the main thing on it was sports, sports, and more sports! He'd been absolutely serious when he'd said he wanted to hear Ashley's surfing pointers. After that, though, the conversation had definitely deteriorated.

Dave *was* an incredibly nice guy. But when she got right down to it, it was pretty easy for Ashley to see the two of them didn't have all that much in common.

"You must have a favorite sport," she said now, deciding to make an effort to meet him halfway.

"No two ways about it," Dave said at once, his voice and face growing animated. "Football."

As she listened to Dave go on happily about the attributes of his favorite sport, Ashley felt herself relax. Now that she understood him, she knew the evening would turn out just fine. Now all she had to do was to make things right with Zoe. . . .

•   •   •

"Anybody home?" Mary-Kate sang out, as she let herself in the townhouse.

Her only answer was the sound of a driving bass beat drifting down the stairs. *Zoe,* she thought. As she hurried toward the kitchen, Mary-Kate checked her watch. The film festival would start in another forty-five minutes. If only Leslie was home, they might still be able to . . .

Mary-Kate pushed open the swinging kitchen door, took two steps into the kitchen, then stopped short. Leslie and a dark-haired girl were standing at the far end of the room, locked in an embrace. At the sight of Mary-Kate they sprang apart. Leslie knocked against the table in the eating nook. An open bottle of soda began to sway dangerously from side to side.

"Oops!" Mary-Kate said, backing up so quickly that the door caught her on its return swing. "Ow! Timing, bad. Mary-Kate leaving now, good. Just pretend I was never here, all right?" Mary-Kate dashed back into the living room.

"Wait, Mary-Kate!" she heard Leslie say in a strangled voice. Whether he was choked up with laughter or embarrassment, she couldn't quite tell. And she really wasn't all that keen on sticking around to find out.

"I'd really like you to meet Theresa," Leslie went on, raising his voice slightly.

Mary-Kate stopped. *What is wrong with me?* she thought. Leslie was her housemate. He'd been totally great about, well, everything. And she was going to express her appreciation by—what? Freaking out? And over what, precisely? For all she knew, he'd been kissing girls all over campus! And why did that thought suddenly make her sick to her stomach?

Trevor. His name popped into her head at that moment.

Just turn around, Mary-Kate, she told herself.

Slowly she retraced her steps into the kitchen. "Is it safe?" she inquired.

"I promise," Leslie replied with a twinkle in his eye. "Mary-Kate, this is Theresa. Theresa, Mary-Kate. You probably met the other night at the party."

"Right, sure, nice to see you again," Mary-Kate said, though she was pretty sure she'd never seen Theresa before.

"You, too," Theresa said.

"Well . . ." Mary-Kate went on. If she'd ever felt more awkward lately, she sure couldn't remember when. "I've got things to do. I'd better run."

"Where to?" Leslie asked.

"There's a film festival starting tonight," Mary-Kate answered, somewhat reluctant now. "The first one's *Breakfast at Tiffany's.* I just came home to see if anybody else felt like going."

"Wow, *Breakfast at Tiffany's.* That's my favorite," Leslie said.

Figures, Mary-Kate thought.

Leslie swiveled his head between the two girls in a way that reminded Mary-Kate of a spectator at a tennis match. "Maybe we could all go?"

Not in this lifetime, Mary-Kate thought.

"You guys go ahead," she answered. "I just remembered something I need to do at home. Have a great time. Nice to see you again, Theresa."

Suddenly desperate to be alone, she sprinted for the privacy of her bedroom and closed the door behind her.

Madison_Ave invites Mary***Kate to Instant Message!

> Madison_Ave: Hey, u. How's it going?
>   Things any better at home?
> Mary***Kate: Can't say for sure. No
>   sightings of the reluctant roomie.
>   Can we talk later?
> Madison_Ave: OK. Over and out.

CHAPTER TWELVE

Thanks a lot for dinner, Dave," Ashley said as they approached the townhouse. "I had fun."

And she really had, she thought. Once she'd gotten a handle on what was really going on between them, Ashley had been able to relax and enjoy herself with Dave.

"Me, too," Dave said. He hesitated for a moment as they stood on the sidewalk.

"You don't have to walk me to the door," Ashley said with a quick laugh.

Dave's handsome face relaxed into a smile. "But I can still try for a good-night kiss, can't I?"

"I don't know. Can you?" Ashley asked, her voice warm.

"Only if you close your eyes," Dave said.

"Very smooth," Ashley said as she obliged. There was no harm in a good-night kiss, she thought. It would be the perfect test of her current theory about her relationship with Dave.

His lips were warm and firm on hers. *Nice!* Ashley

thought. But nothing to rock her theory on its foundations. She and Dave might become friends but nothing more.

"So," Dave said when the kiss was over. "I guess I'll see you around."

"I'm sure you will," Ashley agreed. "Thanks again, Dave."

She watched as he ambled off down the street. Then she turned toward the townhouse. *Well, that's that,* she thought. Now all she had to do was . . .

Halfway through her turn, Ashley stopped short. Now that she was facing the row of townhouses, she could see that she was being watched by two pairs of eyes. One set belonged to the next-door neighbor. The other set belonged to . . . Zoe! She was watching from the bedroom window that overlooked the street, making no effort to hide the fact that she was there.

I have had just about enough, Ashley thought. For better or worse, it was time to have it out with Zoe!

Briskly Ashley marched up the front walk and inserted her key into the door. She let herself into the house, then took the stairs two at a time.

"I have a great idea for your Christmas wish list," she announced as she walked into the bedroom. Zoe was sitting at her desk as if she'd been working. "A pair of binoculars."

"I don't know what you mean," Zoe said without turning around.

Ashley tossed her purse onto her bed. "Come on, Zoe. It's pretty obvious that you don't think much of me, but I'm not stupid, and I'm certainly not blind. I saw you watching me and Dave, and you know it. So let's just stop the games. What you did was rude and inconsiderate. Haven't you ever heard of privacy?"

"You mean like not eavesdropping on people's private phone calls? Things like that?" Zoe retorted as she finally turned around.

"Yes, I heard you on the phone the other day," Ashley admitted. "But there's a difference between that and what you just did. I didn't *intend* to eavesdrop, Zoe. But you deliberately chose to spy on me and Dave."

"You were standing on a public sidewalk making total spectacles of yourselves," Zoe shot back. "I hardly think observing that qualifies as spying."

"The point I'm trying to make here," Ashley said, struggling for self-control, "is that your actions were deliberate. You don't have to like me any more than I have to like you, but as long as we share a room, we have to respect each other's privacy."

Zoe's expression turned stricken. She blinked rapidly, and Ashley was astonished to see that her eyes were filled with tears.

"You don't like me," Zoe whispered.

"That's not what I said," Ashley began.

"You know what? Just save it!" Zoe snapped. She

sprang to her feet and headed for the door. "You've made your feelings about having me as a roommate perfectly clear. You want some privacy? I'm happy to oblige!"

With that, she yanked open the bedroom door, then slammed it behind her, leaving Ashley alone.

"Hello?" An unfamiliar voice sounded in Mary-Kate's ear.

An unfamiliar voice of the female variety.

Mary-Kate jerked her cell phone away from her ear, then punched the OFF button. She sat still for a minute, her heart racing. What was a girl doing answering Trevor's phone?

Okay, Mary-Kate, just get a grip. If Leslie were here, no doubt he'd tell her not to panic. There was probably a perfectly simple explanation, just like the last time. At the thought of Leslie, an odd bubble of emotion rose in Mary-Kate's chest. Quickly she hit REDIAL.

"This is Trevor," his familiar voice said. "Speak now, or forever hold your peace."

Relief spurted through Mary-Kate's entire body. "Trevor, it's Mary-Kate," she said. A big burst of laughter sounded in the background, followed by a scratchy sound she assumed was Trevor muffling the phone against his chest. She heard his voice indistinctly, then he came back on the line.

"I'm sorry, I couldn't hear you," he said.

"Trevor, it's me. Mary-Kate," she said. "Mary-Kate *Olsen*? You remember me?"

"What are you talking about? Of course I remember you," Trevor said.

She heard a second burst of laughter in the background, followed by the quick blast of the stereo.

"Look, Mary-Kate, I'm really sorry, but do you think you could call back later?" Trevor asked. "It's kind of hard to talk at the moment. Max and I got a new mini-fridge, and I think our entire floor just showed up to check it out."

"Okay. Sure. I understand," Mary-Kate said. "You live on a coed floor? When were you going to mention that?"

"What's that supposed to mean?" Trevor asked.

"I'm just wondering why I only hear girls in the background."

"It's a coed school, Mary-Kate," Trevor said evenly. "So is yours, unless I'm mistaken. You're telling me you haven't met any new guys?"

"You've met someone new," Mary-Kate said. She fought to keep her voice calm even as a fireball erupted in her stomach. "You've been at college less than a week, and you've met somebody new. Is that what you're saying, Trev?"

"Of course not," Trevor protested at once. "What I'm saying is . . . " He was drowned out by a sudden upsurge in the volume of the stereo. "Look, could we please talk about this later?" Trevor asked. "I can barely hear you. Things are just too crazy here right now."

"You want to talk later? Fine!" Mary-Kate said. "No, you know what? On second thought, don't worry about it. *You* call *me* whenever you can fit me into your busy social schedule, Trevor. If I'm not here, I'm sure you can handle the enormous disappointment!"

"Wait, Mary-Kate! I—"

Mary-Kate cut him off, then threw the cell phone onto the bed. *Those magazine articles don't know the half of it,* she thought glumly. *Long-distance relationships weren't just tough. They were impossible!*

Mary★★★Kate invites AshleyO to Instant Message!

```
Mary***Kate: Hey, sis. Where are U?
AshleyO: Out wandering. townhouse too
    depressing. Big meltdown with Zoe.
Mary***Kate: Bummer. Wanna talk about
    it?
AshleyO: Maybe when I get back, OK?
Mary***Kate: OK. Remember, u can always
    count on me.
AshleyO: I know.  U too!
Mary***Kate: I know!
```

CHAPTER THIRTEEN

Ashley was exhausted. She'd roamed the campus for what felt like hours, trying to sort out her troubles. Finally she'd headed back to the townhouse. If there was one thing Ashley knew, it was that, while you could occasionally take a time-out, running away from your problems never solved them.

Was I just naïve about how things would be at college? she wondered now, as, on impulse, she sat down on the front steps of the townhouse. The evening had turned chilly, but Ashley just didn't feel ready to go back inside yet. How had things between her and Zoe gone so wrong? And over the oldest conflict in the book: a guy! Sure, there had been other things—the loud music and Zoe's claiming everything in sight before Ashley had even arrived. The truth was, she and Zoe would probably always compete about some things. As their academic backgrounds showed, they were an awful lot alike.

Was Ashley so accustomed to going after what she wanted that she couldn't make a new friend? Now, *there* was an uncomfortable thought!

A quick gust of wind swept the street, making Ashley shiver as fingers of cold air penetrated her lightweight jacket. *I should go inside,* she thought. But she couldn't bring herself to do it. Not quite yet. Instead, she sat on the front steps, gazing up at the stars.

No two ways about it. I'm totally bummed, Mary-Kate thought. There were many ways to handle the situation, but only one seriously appealed to her at the moment.

Ice-cream therapy.

I really hope nobody else snuck in and polished off my container of Chunky Monkey, she thought. Though, if that *had* happened, the offending household member would have taken a major risk. Mary-Kate had labeled the container with her name, then put a skull and crossbones on it, a warning of what would happen if anybody else so much as touched it.

Excellent! It's still here, she thought as a blast of icy air from the freezer poured over her. She fished the ice cream out, then set it on the counter while she rummaged in a cabinet for a bowl and a drawer for a spoon. *This event calls for a* big *spoon,* she decided. *Actually, forget about the bowl. Desperate times call for desperate measures,* she thought. She was simply going to devour her therapy directly from the carton.

She had the first enormous bite halfway to her mouth

when the kitchen door swung open. Mary-Kate's spoon stopped short of her mouth. *Please let that be a girl,* she thought. Across the length of the kitchen, she met Leslie's blue eyes.

"Uh-oh," he said, his tone serious though his eyes invited Mary-Kate to lighten up. "I sense ice-cream therapy is about to begin. Tough night?"

In spite of herself Mary-Kate huffed out a laugh. She set her full spoon back down inside the carton.

"You recognize the signs, huh?"

Leslie nodded as he came all the way into the kitchen, the door swinging closed with a *shush* behind him.

"My sisters' favorites were Cherry Garcia, Chubby Hubby, and Heavenly Hash. That's in chronological order from oldest to youngest sister."

"It helps to have good taste under pressure," Mary-Kate said.

"Absolutely," Leslie said solemnly. He hesitated for a moment, as if uncertain of his standing. "I don't suppose you'd care to share?" he asked. "I'm partial to Chunky Monkey myself."

"This is just your feeble attempt to get me to have only a bowlful. You can't fool me."

"There I go, being transparent again."

Mary-Kate actually produced a small smile. All of a sudden, she discovered she was feeling much better.

"Okay," she said. "Grab a bowl, and sit down."

"All right if I get a spoon, too?"

This time Mary-Kate smiled in earnest. "Suit yourself."

A moment later the two were eating ice cream.

"So," Leslie said, "you want to tell me about it?"

"Only if you tell me about Theresa," Mary-Kate blurted out. Then she blushed. "I'm sorry," she said. "I don't know what made me say that. It's really none of my business."

Leslie was silent for a moment, poking at the ice cream in his bowl with the tip of his spoon. "It's all right," he said. "I don't mind talking about her. But there's nothing much to tell. I met her at the party at the student union. She seemed nice, so I invited her to ours. I like her, but . . . I'm not sure I'm going to pursue anything."

"Why not?" Mary-Kate inquired.

"Uh-uh," Leslie said with a quick shake of his head. "Your turn."

Mary-Kate sighed. "I totally blew up at Trevor," she acknowledged. "You know—my boyfriend in California? I called when he and his roommate had some people over. It was hard to have a conversation, so Trevor asked if I'd call him back, and I completely lost it. In my own defense I have to say that the first time I called, a girl answered the phone."

"What first time?" Leslie asked, sounding confused.

"I called twice. The first time a girl answered the phone. I freaked and hung up, then called back. That was when I lost it and made a fool of myself."

"A 'lost it' *and* a 'freak out'," Leslie commented. He raised a spoonful of ice cream in Mary-Kate's direction as if in salute. "And yet you shared your ice cream. You're an impressive girl, Mary-Kate Olsen."

"I am not. I'm a mess!" Mary-Kate declared, on the verge of tears. "I thought I could handle a long-distance relationship. So far all I've done is lose it, freak, and panic. I haven't even been able to go a week without screwing things up."

"Maybe this first week will be the hardest," Leslie suggested quietly. "You really care about this guy, right?"

"Right," Mary-Kate said as Trevor's image swam into her mind. "He was my best friend before we started dating."

"So why don't you just cut yourself—and him—some slack? Anything that important to you is worth not giving up on."

"You're right. You're absolutely right," Mary-Kate said.

"Besides, it's hard to think straight when you're under pressure," Leslie said.

"How come you're so smart all of a sudden?" Mary-Kate asked.

Leslie shrugged. "I took vitamins as a child."

"You still haven't answered *my* question," Mary-Kate said as she watched him take another bite of ice cream. "Why do you think there's no future for you and Theresa?"

Leslie was quiet for a moment. "I think it's related to the fact that I'm attracted to someone else," he finally acknowledged. "Someone who's not really available at the moment."

Omigosh. He means me! Mary-Kate realized.

The funny feeling in her stomach was back, only this time it didn't feel like a fireball. It felt like butter-flies. She could feel Leslie's blue eyes upon her, com-pelling her to meet them.

He wants to kiss me, she thought. She finally found the courage to look into his eyes.

In the sudden silence of the kitchen the sound of the front door closing was as loud as a gunshot.

"Hello?" a female voice called out. "Anybody home?"

"That's Ashley," Mary-Kate croaked.

Leslie stood up quickly and moved to the sink to rinse his empty bowl. "You might want to go see if she's okay," he suggested. "I thought I heard her and Zoe sort of getting into it earlier."

"Oh, no." Mary-Kate moaned. Quickly she got to her feet to wash her own dish.

"Thanks for the ice cream," Leslie said.

"You're welcome," Mary-Kate said. "Leslie, I—"

The soft *shush* of the kitchen door cut her off before she could finish. By the time she turned around, Leslie was gone.

"I feel like an idiot," Mary-Kate said.

From her position flopped across Madison's bed, Ashley gave an understanding smile. The two had gone to Mary-Kate's room, which they knew would be available since Madison was still at work. There, each had given the other a quick rundown of all the things that had so suddenly gone awry.

"At least that makes two of us," Ashley answered.

"Aha!" Mary-Kate said, sitting up a little straighter on her own bed. "So it's a sister thing. Maybe I can use this to my advantage and make everything your fault?"

"Only if I get to do the same thing," Ashley replied.

The girls fell silent, gazing glumly at each other.

"I guess we really blew it, huh?" Mary-Kate said quietly after a moment. "So much for being independent while away at college. Are we pathetic losers, or what?"

Ashley gave an unexpected laugh at the extremeness of her sister's declaration. Leave it to Mary-Kate to go right to, then over, the top.

"I don't know if I'd go that far," she said. "We've only been here a couple of days, after all. I just think . . . well, I don't know quite what I think. And I think that's the problem."

"Way too much thinking over there!" Mary-Kate said.

"That would be my point."

"No, seriously, Ash," Mary-Kate said, sitting up all the way. "Maybe, away from familiar things, we've both just sort of gone into autopilot mode. You always need to have a plan, to have things go just the way you expect them to."

"What's wrong with that?" Ashley asked, slightly stung.

"Not a thing," Mary-Kate said quickly. "It just can't happen that way all the time. Maybe if you lightened up a little more, things with Zoe would get better."

"I thought you wanted me to stand up for myself!" Ashley protested.

"I did . . . then," Mary-Kate replied. "Now I'm saying you should back off. Maybe you guys weren't meant to hit it off right away like Madison and I did. Maybe you just need to give it some time."

"But I wanted it to be that way," Ashley said mournfully.

"I know you did," Mary-Kate said sympathetically. "But . . ."

"Don't tell me. That would be *your* point!"

"Something along those lines," Mary-Kate acknowledged.

"What's going on with you and Leslie?" Ashley suddenly asked.

Mary-Kate colored. "Me and Leslie?" she responded weakly. "I didn't say anything about Leslie."

"I know you didn't," Ashley said. "But maybe you ought to. You can't fool me, Mary-Kate. You two definitely have a vibe. Maybe the reason you're so freaked about Trevor is because you're afraid *he's* doing the vibe with someone else, too."

Mary-Kate wrinkled her nose. "You make it sound like the latest dance craze or something."

Ashley chuckled. "Okay, so maybe it wasn't the greatest choice of words. But you know what I mean. You think Leslie's cute. Admit it. And if you *weren't* in love with Trevor, you might do something about it."

"That's a pretty big *if*," Mary-Kate countered.

"You're absolutely right," Ashley acknowledged. "But it's an *if* that's definitely out there. And *if* you ask me, the reason you keep blowing up at Trevor is that you're afraid he's having the same experience you are. One that has the potential to make both of you wonder whether or not this long-distance commitment thing is really such a good idea."

"But I love Trevor!" Mary-Kate protested. "I would never want to hurt him."

"And I'm sure he feels the same way about you," Ashley said reassuringly. "In fact, that could be part of the problem. Neither of you wants to hurt the other, but you both perceive the same challenge. You just don't want to admit it yet."

"I thought talking to you was supposed to make me feel better," Mary-Kate commented.

"I'm just telling you what I see," Ashley said. "The same as you did. That doesn't make me right, though I do think you should consider it."

"I will if you will," Mary-Kate promised.

"Deal," Ashley said. She stood up and stretched. "What a day! I'm heading for bed. And, for once, I hope I don't have to sleep with a pillow over my head!"

AshleyO invites Claude18 and Felicity_girl to Instant Message!

AshleyO: Hey, buds back home!

Claude18: Hey, east coast college girl. What's going on?

AshleyO: Thought u might want to drop MK a line. Things are kind of weird with Trevor. She's feeling bummed.

Felicity_girl: Oh no! We will definitely be there for her.

AshleyO: Thanks, guys. I knew I could count on u.

Mary***Kate invites Felicity_girl and Claude18 to Instant Message!

Mary***Kate: Okay, U 2. Stop partying and listen up!

Felicity_girl: Party pooper!

Claude18: What's up?

Mary***Kate: Ashley's definitely having roommate troubles. She's feeling kinda down. A little friendly contact might be just the thing.

Claude18: Really? Imagine that!

Mary***Kate: ??

Felicity-girl: Never mind her. We're on it!

CHAPTER FOURTEEN

Well, I, for one, will be relieved when classes start," Ashley said the following morning. "I'd kind of like to get settled into a regular routine."

"I know just what you mean," Zoe commented.

Ashley sent her a quick, surprised smile. Not only had the music not been on when she'd finally gone up to bed, but her first words with Zoe this morning had been an agreement!

Zoe smiled back, then stared down into her cereal bowl.

From across the breakfast table Madison gave a groan.

"You two are exactly the kind who foul up the test curves for all the rest of us," she proclaimed. "But I'm going to do my best to like you in spite of your obvious shortcomings."

"They can't help it," Mary-Kate confided. "It's this little problem called overachiever syndrome."

The four female housemates were sitting around the breakfast table, discussing their plans for the day, most of which involved class registration. Honest-to-goodness college life would begin in just a few more days. Just that morning their RA had phoned to say they could officially become dorm residents the day after tomorrow.

Before either Ashley or Zoe could protest Mary-Kate's remark, they heard the sound of the front door opening and closing.

"That must be Leslie," Madison said. "He said he was heading out for a run."

No sooner had she finished speaking than a breathless Leslie appeared in the kitchen doorway. "Hey, gang, we'd better get a move on. The registration lines are really long already."

"But registration doesn't even officially start until ten o'clock," Ashley protested.

But Leslie was already heading off toward the den. "You know what they say about the early bird," he called back over his shoulder.

"I hear that," Ashley said. She shot to her feet. "Thank goodness I know exactly what classes I want. All I have to do is get my notes."

"They're right in the center of your desk," Zoe said as she got to her feet, too. "I remember noticing yours because that's where I put mine!"

"I like to be prepared," Ashley said as, together, the two roommates dashed up the stairs.

Zoe nodded vigorously. "I couldn't agree with you more!"

•   •   •

I am now officially ready for this to be over, Mary-Kate thought as she listened to her stomach growl. It was time for lunch! Between one class registration location and another, she had spent her entire morning standing in various lines.

The only good thing about the situation was that, so far, Mary-Kate was getting all the classes she wanted. Also this eternal standing around was giving her lots of time to give the situation with Trevor a good mental going-over.

The trouble was, the longer Mary-Kate thought, the more she had to admit that Ashley had been right. In spite of her commitment to Trevor, Mary-Kate was very definitely attracted to Leslie.

What's not to like? she thought now as her current line inched forward. *He's nice. He's smart. He's funny. And then there are those blue eyes.*

A girl would have to be lacking a pulse *not* to find a combination like that attractive, even if she *was* devoted to another guy. The question was, did noticing Leslie make her a complete and total jerk? Did it make her untrue to Trevor in her heart?

"Hey!" A familiar voice broke into her troubled thoughts. "How's it going?"

Grateful to have a break from her uncomfortable musings, Mary-Kate turned to find Madison by her side.

"Not too bad," she admitted. "If you're talking about the line situation. This is my last one."

"I'm all through," Madison announced. "I got lucky. I got everything I wanted."

"That's great!" Mary-Kate said. "Congratulations."

"How about if I hang with you until you're done here?" Madison suggested. "Make the last wait seem shorter."

"I won't say no to that suggestion," Mary-Kate said.

Again, the line moved forward.

"What did you mean earlier?" Madison suddenly asked her.

Mary-Kate's brow wrinkled. "Earlier when?"

"Just a minute ago, when I asked how things were going. You said the line situation wasn't bad. That tells me you've got something else on your mind. I'd go ahead and spill it if I were you. I'll weasel it out of you eventually anyhow."

Mary-Kate gave a chuckle. When Madison really wanted something, she was pretty hard to resist. *It might be good to have a fresh perspective,* she decided.

"Hypothetically speaking . . ." she began.

"Oh, I get it," Madison interrupted. "You're going to talk about yourself, but you don't want to admit it. Okay, go on."

"You keep interrupting me," Mary-Kate said.

Madison grinned and made a zipping motion to show that her lips were sealed.

"As I was saying, hypothetically speaking . . . " Mary-Kate said once more. "Say there's this girl who's in love. The trouble is, her true love happens to be all the way across the country. Far away from her guy and in a new situation, our girl suddenly she discovers she's attracted to another guy. Would you say that makes her an untrustworthy creep?"

"Not necessarily," Madison replied. "Has this girl acted on her attraction? I mean, has she actually gone back on her word to her true love?"

"No, she hasn't," Mary-Kate answered honestly, genuinely relieved that that was her reply. "But the whole situation makes her feel pretty weirded out and confused."

"That sounds only natural," Madison commented. She was silent for a moment as the line advanced yet again. Now Mary-Kate was only third from the front of the line.

"I guess I'd tell this hypothetical girl to lighten up a little," Madison went on at last. "It sounds as if she might be overanalyzing things. Maybe she should just relax and go with the flow."

"But—" Mary-Kate began. But the line gave a quick surge, and suddenly the registration desk was before her.

"Name and student ID number, please," a harassed-looking administrative assistant said.

Quickly Mary-Kate pulled her thoughts back to the matter at hand. Important as getting her emotional life sorted out was, there was one other little thing she was supposed to be doing. Say, for instance, actually attending college!

I did it! Ashley thought as she let herself in the townhouse. *Let's hear it for being organized!*

By dint of much hustling, Ashley was now enrolled in every single class she wanted. Getting into English 101 had been her final accomplishment. She'd been the next to the last name to make it in. Talk about the nick of time!

Halfway up the stairs to her room, Ashley heard the sound of the stereo booming to life. But it didn't sound like Zoe's usual choice of sixties rock. In fact, unless Ashley was very much mistaken, it was . . .

"Isn't that the soundtrack to *Lord of the Rings*?" she asked as she reached the bedroom.

Zoe jumped. "I didn't hear you come in."

"Sorry," Ashley replied. "I honestly didn't mean to startle you. Guess I came in during a loud part. *Lord of the Rings,* right?"

"Right." Zoe nodded, her expression brightening. "I don't usually go for soundtracks," she went on. "But the truth is . . ." She gave a sigh and shook her head. "The truth is going to make me sound like a total nutball. Sometimes I put this on and think about—"

"Orlando Bloom!" Ashley said before Zoe could finish.

"That's it exactly!" Zoe said. She sat up straight. "How did you know?"

Ashley put her hands on her hips and regarded her roommate severely. "You have got to be kidding, right? How many different ways can you say *duh*?"

At the unexpectedness of Ashley's response, Zoe broke into gales of delighted laughter.

That's the first time I've heard her do that, Ashley thought. "There's something funny about Orlando Bloom?" Ashley asked.

"No, no, it's not that," Zoe said as she wiped her streaming eyes.

Ashley sat down on her own bed. From across the room the two girls faced each other.

"It's just that I never figured you for the mooning-over-movie-stars type," Zoe said.

"Well, one has to be selective," Ashley said, as if this was simply common sense. "I don't do it for just anyone."

"Absolutely not," Zoe agreed at once.

The two shared a conspiratorial smile.

This is just the way I wanted things to be, Ashley thought. She pulled in a deep and silent breath.

"Zoe," she said, her tone serious. "I owe you an apology. I got totally weirded out over the situation with Dave Calhoun, and I behaved like a jerk. I'm sorry. The truth is, I really want us to be friends. Do you suppose we could, you know, start over, or something?"

Zoe was silent for a moment, staring down at her hands clasped tightly in her lap. "Why?" she asked suddenly.

"Well, I was rude, and I want to make things right," Ashley said.

"That's not what I mean," Zoe said with a quick shake of her head. "I mean, why do you want to be friends with me, Ashley?"

"Why wouldn't I want to be your friend?" Ashley asked, genuinely puzzled. "We're roommates. We're going to be together all year. It's self-defense, if nothing else."

Zoe's lips curled in a slow smile. "But if we weren't roommates," she said, "would you still want to be my friend?"

"That's not a question I can answer, Zoe," Ashley said honestly. "The whole reason we met is because we *are* roommates. And because of that, I want us to be friends. I've been looking forward to being best buds with my college roomie ever since I first applied."

"Me, too," Zoe said. All of a sudden her words began to tumble over one another as if, now that she'd decided to speak, she couldn't get them out fast enough.

"But then, that first day, when I saw you, you looked so—I don't know—perfect or something. And you already had Mary-Kate. Everybody knows how sisters bond. I just couldn't figure out how I would ever fit into that. Geez, do I sound like a pathetic loser or what?"

"You're not a loser," Ashley said quickly. "Any more than I'm perfect. I would have thought you'd have noticed that by now. What I am is the same thing you are—living away from home for the first time. I figure that means I need all the new friends I can get. That includes you."

"I'd like that, too," Zoe said. "I'm sorry about how I behaved before. The truth is, I really sort of fell for Dave. But I couldn't figure why he'd look at me twice when you were around."

"Don't be ridiculous," Ashley said. "Actually, I think you guys have a lot more in common than Dave and I do. You actually play some of those sports he's always talking about!"

"So you wouldn't mind if we, you know, really started going out?"

"Absolutely not," Ashley said. "In fact, I'd be happy for you. He's a nice guy. There is just one thing, though."

"What's that?" Zoe asked.

"Do you suppose we could start this CD over from the beginning? That way we could share all our favorite Orlando moments."

"Absolutely!" Zoe said. With a laugh she jumped up from the bed and headed for the stereo.

Finally! Ashley thought as the opening strains of

the soundtrack began to fill the room. Not only had she and Zoe settled their differences, they were well on their way to bonding.

"Here's to successfully making it through registration!" Mary-Kate proclaimed. She lifted her orange juice glass high in a toast.

Around the kitchen table the housemates clinked glasses. It was hard for Mary-Kate to believe, but this was actually their first meal all together since they'd moved into the townhouse. To celebrate, the sisters had mixed up a batch of their mom's world-famous pancakes. Who cared if it was actually lunch?

"These are so good!" Zoe exclaimed as she took her final bite. "I'd love to eat that last one, but if I do, I'm afraid I'll explode!"

"A familiar dilemma," Leslie agreed. "To overindulge or not to overindulge." He speared the last pancake remaining on the serving platter and quickly transferred it to his plate. "Fortunately for the rest of you, I am prepared to make the supreme sacrifice."

"Mighty big of you," Madison commented.

"Mmm," Leslie said around a mouthful of pancake. "That's just what I'm afraid of."

As she joined in the general laughter, Mary-Kate saw his blue eyes twinkling at her.

"So," Ashley said briskly as she pushed her plate away. "Did everybody get the classes they wanted?"

A chorus of nods and yeses greeted her question.

"Though I do have to say the morning had its challenging moments," Leslie commented now that his mouth wasn't quite so full. "Not just the standing in line. Some of those course letters look awfully alike. I almost ended up in Basket Weaving 101."

Mary-Kate took Leslie's schedule from the pile in the center of the table. "BW 101. If that's not basket weaving, what on earth is that?"

"Basic waltzing," Leslie replied.

Zoe gave a sputter of laughter that sounded dangerously like she was choking on her OJ. Ashley thumped her on the back while the rest of the table roared.

"Biology workshop," Leslie admitted. "It's sort of a study group outside of the regular lab work."

"I didn't know you were interested in engineering, Ashley," Madison said, as she looked over Ashley's schedule.

Ashley stopped thumping Zoe, who had completely recovered. "That's because I'm not. What makes you think I am?"

Madison held the schedule out across the table toward her. "Because you signed up for Engineering 101. See? Right there on the bottom."

"No way," Ashley protested at once. "That's English 101."

"I really hate to break this to you," Zoe said, "but

it's not. The code for that is *EGL* 101, not *ENG* 101. You wanted Professor Drake, just like I did, right?" She proffered her own schedule as evidence.

"Omigosh!" Ashley said. "This is terrible. I signed up for the wrong course!"

"It'll be okay," Mary-Kate said swiftly as she looked at both Madison and Leslie for support. "The registrar's office is still open. I'm sure if you go over there right now, you can straighten the whole thing out."

"I hope so," Ashley said, jumping up.

"Don't worry about cleaning up," Zoe put in as Ashley quickly carried her plate to the sink. "I'll handle that. You just get over to the registrar's office."

"Thanks. I appreciate it," Ashley said.

"Don't hesitate to call for reinforcements if you need help," Mary-Kate said. But she wasn't all that sure Ashley heard her. She was already running for the door.

Mary***Kate invites Madison_Ave to Instant Message!

```
Mary***Kate: Hey. U noticing what I'm
    noticing?
Madison_Ave: If it's about Ashley and
    Zoe, the answer is yes, yes, yes!
    What happened? Do u know?
Mary***Kate: Nope. Just happy things
    seem better.
Madison_Ave: That makes 2 of us!
```

CHAPTER FIFTEEN

Several frustrating hours later Ashley sat in the student union, trying to get a handle on her disappointment. She'd arrived at the registrar's office only to be informed that the class she wanted was completely full. The only one who could approve her entry at this point was Professor Drake himself.

Praying that the professor was the understanding, flexible type, Ashley had hurried directly to his office, only to have complete and utter disaster strike. Professor Drake was the guy who lived in the townhouse next door! He'd taken one look at Ashley and turned her down flat. Ashley hadn't even tried to plead her case. She'd known it was hopeless.

Maybe it's for the best, she told herself now. Professor Drake wasn't the only one who taught English 101. But student gossip had it that Drake was the best. He made you work hard, but you learned a lot—precisely the experience Ashley wanted. She didn't want to start out her college career by taking second best. Unfortunately, it didn't look as if she had a choice.

"Hey, Ashley, what's the matter? World come to an end?"

Shaken out of her glum thoughts, Ashley looked up to discover that Dave Calhoun had materialized at her side.

"Just about," she told him. "I didn't get into a class I really wanted. English 101 with Professor Drake."

A strange expression crossed Dave's face as he sat down beside her. "Isn't he supposed to be the hardest?"

"Yep," Ashley said. "That's why I wanted him. It's just a general survey, but it's supposed to really prepare you for upper division courses."

"Okay, I have to say this," Dave said after a moment. "You are totally blowing my mind. I'd never get upset over not getting a particular class, let alone a hard one!"

"But you *would* get upset if you didn't get the coach or make the team you really wanted, wouldn't you?" Ashley countered.

Dave nodded, his expression thoughtful. "Good point," he acknowledged.

All of a sudden he stood up. "Also a good thing that you know me," he said, his eyes laughing. "I might be able to help."

"What? How?" Ashley demanded.

"Let me check it out and get back to you," Dave said. Then he walked off, leaving Ashley staring after him.

Wouldn't it be amazing if Dave turned out to be her hero the very day after she'd decided to give him up to Zoe?

"Mary-Kate?"

"Trevor!" Mary-Kate exclaimed breathlessly as she answered the ring of her cell phone. The sound of his voice filled her with happiness and trepidation all at the same time. What on earth was she going to say after the way she'd behaved?

"I was just thinking about you. This is so great," she said.

"I've been thinking about you, too," Trevor said. "A lot. Look, I just want to get this out of the way right off, okay? I'm sorry about the other night. It really was a bad time, but I should have handled the situation better."

"I'm sorry, too," Mary-Kate said. "I didn't handle things very well either. I didn't mean to lose my temper, it's just . . ."

How can I explain? she wondered. Then she remembered that this was Trevor. They'd been best buds before they'd been sweethearts. Next to Ashley, there was no one in the world Mary-Kate trusted more.

"I'm finding this whole long-distance relationship thing tougher than I thought," she said quickly before she could lose her nerve. "I thought I understood how to make it work. But now that I'm actually here, I'm not so sure anymore. The only thing I am sure of is that I love you and I don't ever want to hurt you."

There was a heartbeat of silence.

"You've been doing it again, haven't you?" Trevor asked.

"What?"

"Reading my mind. The reason I didn't call you back before now is that I've been racking my brain, trying to figure out how to tell you exactly what you just told me."

"Did it hurt?" Mary-Kate inquired. She was rewarded when Trevor gave a chuckle.

"The whole thing hurts," he answered honestly. "And it confuses me. I guess the bottom line is, I feel like there are so many new things coming at me at once, it would be better if I could just concentrate on the here and now. It's not that I want to see other people or that I want us to break up," he added quickly.

"I know what you mean, Trevor," Mary-Kate assured him softly. "I feel like I'm being pulled in a hundred different directions and that soon I'll start to resent what's pulling me *away* from here. I think that's why I can't seem to get a handle on how this works."

"Boy, you really *are* good," Trevor said.

"So I take it we agree," Mary-Kate said. "We don't split up, but we don't cling either. We take each day as it comes. There are approximately sixty-eight days before Thanksgiving break, by the way. Just in case you want to keep track on your calendar."

Trevor gave a quick chuckle, and Mary-Kate felt her heart click back into place. She loved that sound. The fact that Trevor had laughed told her that everything was going to be all right. They were making the right decision.

"I want to know the minute you book your flight home," he said. "That way I can go camp out at the airport."

"Done," Mary-Kate promised.

"I'll talk to you soon, okay?"

"Okay. Thanks for calling. Trevor, I . . . "

"Same here," he said before she could finish. "And don't worry, Mary-Kate. I'll be here when you get home."

"I'll be counting on it," Mary-Kate said. Her eyes slightly teary, she punched the OFF button on the phone.

She'd done it. She'd told the truth. It looked as if her life at college really was about to start.

Mary***Kate invites AshleyO, Claude18, Felicity_girl, and Madison_Ave to Instant Message!

Mary***Kate: Trevor and I have decided we're just going 2 cool the whole long-distance thing. It's way 2 confusing and hard!

Claude18: But ur not breaking up, right?

Mary***Kate: No way. Just taking the pressure off. Be more chill about meeting new people.

Felicity_girl: Sounds sensible 2 me. What do u think, Ash?

AshleyO: I agree.

Madison_Ave: I have just 1 question.

Mary***Kate: Shoot.

Madison_Ave: Who are all u guys?

CHAPTER SIXTEEN

Y ou're joking!" Zoe exclaimed. "*Dave* saved the day?"

"Absolutely," Ashley said. "In fact, he was nothing less than my knight in shining armor. You know his aunt lives in New York, so he's been here all summer, right?" she asked.

"Actually, I didn't," Zoe admitted. "But go on!"

"Well, apparently Professor Drake's sister and her family live next door to Dave's aunt, and the professor's nephew is totally into—"

"Wait—don't tell me," Zoe interrupted. "Football!"

Ashley nodded. "You got it in one. Dave's been giving the kid football pointers that have really paid off. So when he heard I was in a bind with Drake, he paid his aunt a visit and just sort of dropped in next door. Half an hour later Professor Drake's sister calls him with an urgent request, and, *voilà*!"

She brandished her new schedule in the air like a flag, then set it down on her desk. "Yours truly is now enrolled in *EGL* 101! With Professor Drake."

"Awesome," Zoe commented.

"Of course, I might have to attend class in disguise."

"Oh, hey, I almost forgot!" Zoe exclaimed. "While you were out, Sharon, our RA, dropped by to remind us that we can move into the dorm tomorrow."

"Excellent!" Ashley cried.

"Not only that, but she also complimented us on how well we'd kept up the townhouse. Evidently there haven't been any complaints about us. Maybe Drake is a secret softie."

"I can only wish!" Ashley said.

"Also," Zoe said. "I . . . well . . . I have something for you."

She moved to the chest of drawers she'd claimed the very first day and drew out two tissue-paper wrapped packages from the bottom drawer.

"My mom made these," she said as she handed one to Ashley. "I probably already mentioned that my dad was kind of weird about my going away to college, but my mom was absolutely great about it. She's pretty hot with a sewing machine. She does alterations to help bring in a little extra money. She made these. One for me and one for my roommate. I was going to wait until we moved into the dorm, but I'd like you to have it now."

Ashley opened the wrapping. Inside was a handmade pillowcase, in a great fifties-reproduction fabric depicting students on a college campus. Little vignettes showed guys offering to carry gals' books, and groups of girls slurping malteds at a soda fountain. One girl was even wearing a poodle skirt.

"This is absolutely the best," Ashley said. "What's yours look like?"

"Same fabric only in a different color," Zoe said. She held it out. "So they go together but they're not exactly the same."

"Sort of like roommates," Ashley said with a glow of happiness. "Thanks, Zoe."

"You're welcome," Zoe said with a smile. "Though don't get all mushy on me. I'm still going to fight for the bed by the window."

"That I can deal with," Ashley declared. "Just so long as you don't put those horrible posters on the wall!"

"They really are the worst, aren't they?" Zoe asked. "I guess I got carried away with trying to be cool."

"Hey," Ashley said. "I have an idea. Come on. Let's go."

"Where?" Zoe asked as Ashley grabbed her by the hand and steered her out the door.

"Back to the Shop Mart," Ashley proclaimed. "We can pick out posters together this time. Not only that, but you can also help me pick out the perfect thank-you card for your mom."

"Done!" Zoe said.

The roommates left the townhouse together, arm in arm.

"Hello?" Mary-Kate said tentatively as she knocked on Leslie's door. "Anybody home?"

She was pretty sure there was. Not long after her conversation with Trevor, she thought she'd heard Leslie come in, then head for the den that served as his temporary bedroom.

"Come on in," Leslie called.

Mary-Kate pushed open the door, and walked a short distance into the room. "Hey," she said.

Leslie looked up from where he was arranging items in his oversize duffel bag.

"Hey, yourself. I'm getting a jump-start on my packing here. You know, since we'll be leaving soon, and all."

"I sort of wish we weren't," Mary-Kate said honestly. "I've kind of gotten used to having you around."

"Me, too," Leslie said. He straightened and faced Mary-Kate across the room. "So, how's it going?"

"I straightened things out with Trevor," Mary-Kate said. "We're not going to break up, but we're also not going to put too much pressure on the whole long-distance thing. I guess you could say we compromised."

"Oookaaay," Leslie said, drawing the word out as if he was thinking that over. "Just so I have things straight, does this mean you'd be willing to consider spending time with another guy?"

"Only if he had reasonable expectations," Mary-Kate answered. "He'd have to be willing to take things sort of slow."

"And if he was willing to do that?" Leslie inquired, his blue eyes intent.

"Then I guess there'd be just one more thing that I could think of."

"What?"

"He'd have to ask me first."

Leslie's face blossomed into a smile. "Will you go out with me, Mary-Kate?" he asked. "As long as we don't rush into anything? For example, if I exercised remarkable self-restraint, I think I could wait until tomorrow."

"Tomorrow would be good," Mary-Kate said.

"Okay," Leslie said. "You're on."

As she retraced her steps to Ashley's room for a much needed sister session, Mary-Kate could feel her spirits start to soar.

Tomorrow their first day of college would officially begin. Judging from the events of orientation week, if there was one thing the sisters knew they could count on, it was that college life was most definitely *not* going to be boring.

Just the way they liked things. Full of surprises.

Win the Best Party Ever!

ONE LUCKY WINNER
gets to throw a great party for ten friends!

You receive:
- Karaoke machine
- Fragrance
- Purses
- Cosmetics
- Hair Accessories
- CDs
- Videos

PLUS A $250 GIFT CHECK FOR PARTY FOOD AND GOODIES!

Mail to: **MARY-KATE AND ASHLEY GRADUATION SUMMER SWEEPSTAKES!**
c/o HarperEntertainment
Attention: Children's Marketing Department
10 East 53rd Street, New York, NY 10022

No purchase necessary.

Name:

Address:

City: State: Zip:

Phone: Age:

Mary-Kate and Ashley *Graduation Summer*
Best Party Ever Sweepstakes
OFFICIAL RULES:

1. NO PURCHASE OR PAYMENT NECESSARY TO ENTER OR WIN.

2. How to Enter. To enter, complete the official entry form or hand print your name, address, age and phone number along with the words "Graduation Summer Best Party Ever Sweepstakes" on a 3". x 5" card and mail to: Graduation Summer Best Party Ever Sweepstakes, c/o HarperEntertainment, Attn: Children's Marketing Department, 10 East 53rd Street, New York, NY 10022. Entries must be received no later than November 30, 2004. Enter as often as you wish, but each entry must be mailed separately. One entry per envelope. Partially completed, illegible, or mechanically reproduced entries will not be accepted. Sponsor is not responsible for lost, late, mutilated, illegible, stolen, postage due, incomplete, or misdirected entries. All entries become the property of Dualstar Entertainment Group, LLC, and will not be returned.

3. Eligibility. Sweepstakes open to all legal residents of the United States (excluding Colorado and Rhode Island) who are between the ages of five and fifteen on November 30, 2004 excluding employees and immediate family members of HarperCollins Publishers, Inc., ("HarperCollins"), Parachute Properties and Parachute Press, Inc., and their respective subsidiaries and affiliates, officers, directors, shareholders, employees, agents, attorneys, and other representatives and their immediate families (individually and collectively, "Parachute"), Dualstar Entertainment Group, LLC, and its subsidiaries and affiliates, officers, directors, shareholders, employees, agents, attorneys, and other representatives and their immediate families (individually and collectively, "Dualstar"), and their respective parent companies, affiliates, subsidiaries, advertising, promotion and fulfillment agencies, and the persons with whom each of the above are domiciled. All applicable federal, state and local laws and regulations apply. Offer void where prohibited or restricted by law.

4. Odds of Winning. Odds of winning depend on the total number of entries received. Approximately 300,000 sweepstakes announcements published. All prizes will be awarded. Winner will be randomly drawn on or about December 15, 2004 by HarperCollins, whose decision is final. Potential winner will be notified by mail and will be required to sign and return an affidavit of eligibility and release of liability within 14 days of notification. Prizes won by minors will be awarded to parent or legal guardian who must sign and return all required legal documents. By acceptance of their prize, winner consents to the use of their name, photograph, likeness, and biographical information by HarperCollins, Parachute, Dualstar, and for publicity purposes without further compensation except where prohibited.

5. Grand Prize. One Grand Prize Winner will win one karaoke machine, 10 Mary-Kate and Ashley back-to-school purses containing Mary-Kate and Ashley merchandise (party music CDs, videos, fragrance, cosmetics, hair accessories) and $250 to be used by winner toward the purchase of party goods and food. Approximate combined retail value of prize totals $1000.00.

6. Prize Limitations. All prizes will be awarded. Only one prize will be awarded per individual, family, or household. Prizes are nontransferable and cannot be sold or redeemed for cash. No cash substitute is available. Any federal, state, or local taxes are the responsibility of the winner. Sponsor may substitute prize of equal or greater value, if necessary, due to availability.

7. Additional terms: By participating, entrants agree a) to the official rules and decisions of the judges, which will be final in all respects; and to waive any claim to ambiguity of the official rules and b) to release, discharge, and hold harmless HarperCollins, Warner, Parachute, Dualstar, and their respective parent companies, affiliates, subsidiaries, employees and representatives and advertising, promotion and fulfillment agencies from and against any and all liability or damages associated with acceptance, use, or misuse of any prize received or participation in any Sweepstakes-related activity or participation in this Sweepstakes.

8. Dispute Resolution. Any dispute arising from this Sweepstakes will be determined according to the laws of the State of New York, without reference to its conflict of law principles, and the entrants consent to the personal jurisdiction of the State and Federal courts located in New York County and agree that such courts have exclusive jurisdiction over all such disputes.

9. Winner Information. To obtain the name of the winner, please send your request and a self-addressed stamped envelope (residents of Vermont may omit return postage) to Graduation Summer Best Party Ever Winner, c/o HarperEntertainment, 10 East 53rd Street, New York, NY 10022 by April 1, 2005.

10. Sweepstakes Sponsor: HarperCollins Publishers, Inc.

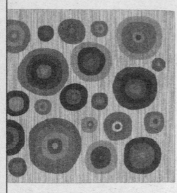